MURDER AT THE FLEA CLUB

MURDER AT THE FLEA CLUB

Matthew Head

FELONY & MAYHEM PRESS • NEW YORK

All the characters and events portrayed in this work are fictitious.

MURDER AT THE FLEA CLUB

A Felony & Mayhem mystery

PRINTING HISTORY
First edition (Simon & Schuster): 1955
Felony & Mayhem edition: 2018

ISBN: 978-1-63194-138-2

Manufactured in the United States of America

Library of Congress Cataloging-in-Publication Data

Names: Head, Matthew, 1907-1985.
Title: Murder at the Flea Club / Matthew Head.
Description: New York : Felony & Mayhem Press, 2018. | "A Felony & Mayhem mystery"
Identifiers: LCCN 2017060959| ISBN 9781631941382 (trade pbk.) | ISBN 9781631941078 (ebook)
Subjects: LCSH: Murder--Investigation--Fiction. | Paris (France)--Fiction. | Mystery fiction.
Classification: LCC PS3505.A53196 M87 2018 | DDC 813/.54--dc23
LC record available at https://lccn.loc.gov/2017060959

Matthew Head is the pseudonym of John Edwin Canaday (1907-1985), an art critic and writer. Canaday was a *New York Times* art critic for seventeen years and authored several monographs of visual art scholarship. Late in life he wrote restaurant reviews for the *Times*. Under the "Matthew Head" pen name, he wrote seven mystery novels, three of which are set in the Congo and based on his experiences traveling there as a French translator in 1943. Canaday was born in Fort Scott, Kansas; his series sleuth, Dr. Mary Finney, is from Fort Scott as well.

The icon above says you're holding a copy of a book in the Felony & Mayhem "Vintage" category. These books were originally published prior to about 1965, and feature the kind of twisty, ingenious puzzles beloved by fans of Agatha Christie and John Dickson Carr. If you enjoy this book, you may well like other "Vintage" titles from Felony & Mayhem Press.

For more about these books, and other Felony & Mayhem titles, or to place an order, please visit our website at:

www.FelonyAndMayhem.com

Other "Vintage" titles from

FELONY & MAYHEM

ANTHONY BERKELEY

The Poisoned Chocolates Case

ELIZABETH DALY

Unexpected Night
Deadly Nightshade
Murders in Volume 2
The House without the Door
Evidence of Things Seen
Nothing Can Rescue Me
Arrow Pointing Nowhere
The Book of the Dead
Any Shape or Form
Somewhere in the House
The Wrong Way Down
Night Walk
The Book of the Lion
And Dangerous to Know
Death and Letters
The Book of the Crime

MATTHEW HEAD

The Devil in the Bush
The Cabinda Affair
The Congo Venus

NGAIO MARSH

A Man Lay Dead
Enter a Murderer
The Nursing Home Murders
Death in Ecstasy
Vintage Murder
Artists in Crime
Death in a White Tie
Overture to Death
Death at the Bar
Surfeit of Lampreys
Death and the Dancing Footman
Colour Scheme
Died in the Wool
Final Curtain
Swing Brother, Swing
Night at the Vulcan
Spinsters in Jeopardy
Scales of Justice
Death of a Fool
Singing in the Shrouds
False Scent
Hand in Glove
Dead Water
Killer Dolphin
Clutch of Constables
When in Rome
Tied Up in Tinsel
Black as He's Painted
Last Ditch
A Grave Mistake
Photo Finish
Light Thickens
Collected Short Mysteries

PATRICIA MOYES

Dead Men Don't Ski
The Sunken Sailor
Death on the Agenda
Murder à la Mode

LENORE GLEN OFFORD

Skeleton Key
The Glass Mask
The Smiling Tiger
My True Love Lies
The 9 Dark Hours

MURDER AT THE FLEA CLUB

CHAPTER ONE

FOR A WHILE I ran this sort of art gallery in Paris. You have to get a year in Paris out of your blood sooner or later, and this seemed to be a good time to do it. I was between jobs. At least I hoped I was between jobs, since I hoped one would materialise in the future, one having terminated in the recent past. I have a small income in any case, and the art gallery broke even, which was a surprise, so I didn't have anything to worry about, really. Altogether it was a pleasant enough year, although I almost froze to death. Three years in the Congo on government assignments taught me how to keep cool in the heat, but they did something to me. I haven't been warm in the cold since.

The African experience was the main reason I started the art gallery. I made a good friend down there, a medical missionary named Dr. Mary Finney, who has acquired a certain secondary reputation as an amateur detective. I never expected to see her in Paris. Her territory covers the rougher parts of the Congo, and in between giving injections to the natives she runs across quite a lot of good stuff in the way of tribal masks and fetishes. She doesn't care anything for these and never did, which was wonderful for me because she would pass them on to me, so that I have really a pretty good collection. That kind of thing sells readily nowadays and I stocked my art gallery with the excess from my own collection, and Dr. Finney kept sending me new things from time to time. Along with this primitive sculpture I had a small stable of starveling painters from neighbouring garrets. It wasn't a bad little art gallery at all.

However, this isn't the story of an art gallery, it's the story of a murder, which occurred at a place called The Flea Club. I should say right now that my name is Hooper Taliaferro, pronounced *Tolliver*, I always have to add. No detailed description of me is necessary. Medium as to looks, intelligence, ambition, and so on, but I get along. My only real talent is as a spectator. I am one of the best people to be found anywhere, when it comes to just watching. It is really my life work.

This was in February. I had just given myself a couple of weeks' vacation and had spent it in Siena, thinking it would be warmer. I nearly froze there too. On the morning I got back to Paris the city was covered with snow. It bleached everything to soft whites and pearly greys; snow lay on the trees along the boulevards so that they receded in diminishing feathery clusters of white; the stone nymphs and goddesses in the Tuileries gardens held snow in great armfuls; along the streets and sidewalks the people and even the automobiles moved slowly and silently.

I walked for a long time with the special feeling of security you get when your coat and hat and overshoes keep you warm and dry against the chill and damp of the surrounding air. All the familiar places were simplified, all their primary accents intensified, by the deposits of snow along their projections. The snow had fallen during the night and now it was continuing into the morning. As I walked it began to stop, until the sky began to clear, with a suggestion of gold here and there where the sun was going to be. Through my glove, with my hand in the pocket of my coat, I could feel the neat angular shapes of two letters, my accumulated mail for the past two weeks. One of them had a Belgian Congo stamp representing an okapi, and the other was from a female cousin in Madison, Wisconsin, with several stamps including profile portraits of some good men—Washington, Jefferson and Adams. One of the letters was going to involve me in the murder at The Flea Club; the other, in its solution.

In winter the cafés enclose their sidewalk areas in glass-paned shelters, and keep a coal-stove burning in there. If you get a table close to the stove, it's really good. I turned now towards the Champs-Elysées, not ordinarily a habitat of mine, but crowded with cafés expensive enough to have good fires. At the far end of the avenue the Arc de Triomphe, usually so substantial, hung like a piece of gauze. In the café there was only a scattering of people, which meant that I would feel free to sit as long as I wanted to, and they were good-looking, well-dressed people, always pleasanter to see in cold weather than the poor.

My female cousin from Madison is not a part of this story, except for the events her letter set in motion. "HOOP DEAR," it began, and then it briefed me on the children's colds for that season, and so forth and so on, and then:

> *Incidentally, do you remember Abby Bingham?* [I did not—or barely did, a small child of no particular individuality who had played with us.] *Hadn't heard from her for years, but she telephoned me the other day passing through town with her husband. Her name is Corbett now and she has four children—imagine, little Abby! We had such a nice talk on the phone. Of course she wanted to know all about you, and she was simply thrilled to hear you were in Paris. It seems a good friend of her sister's is in*

Paris too and Abby thinks you might enjoy meeting somebody from home. [Oddest idea in the world, but everybody has it.] *She is a Mrs. Bellen—a widow if you please and very good-looking, Abby says, so watch your step, eh Hoopy? Seriously, though, Abby would appreciate it if you would look Mrs. Bellen up. She is at something called the Prince du Royaume on the Rue François Premier. Does that make sense? Now this is sort of confused but her daughter is along with her and Abby says please be very tactful because there is something very sad or something. It is really the reason they are in Paris, but I couldn't get it straight on the phone, the daughter is insane or pregnant or something terrible like that, I couldn't get it straight on the phone, Abby was talking so fast and I was so excited hearing from her after all this time. Anyway it is the Mrs. B., not her daughter, that you're supposed to look up. Now you do that, and don't forget us homebodies with all your fancy adventures, and remember I gave Abby my word of honour you would look up Mrs. Bellen. Must stop. Love,* MARGE.

I seldom look up friends of friends, but it was an unusual morning anyway, and the Rue François Premier was near-by. Things happen in such curious ways; certainly Audrey Bellen turned out to be the last person you'd have expected to meet through the connection of a girl like my female cousin. And the Prince du Royaume was a far, far cry from Madison, Wisconsin.

The entrance lobby was as intimate, as chaste, as crystalline, as if it had been carved from a glacier. Here and there the ice was rimmed with gold. Crystal chandeliers released occasional rays of light which shattered against a monumental series of *torchères* in gilt and onyx. The lobby was small, long in proportion to its width, with several small pale draped recesses alongside, suggesting boudoirs. They held a few effectively disposed chairs and tables, Louis XVI, that could have gone into any museum.

In the alcoves the glacial air was relieved. They had been carved not from ice but from rose quartz. The exquisite furniture sat within the pastel glow with the air of aristocrats awaiting the call to the tumbrils.

This little dream world was populated by two people when I entered: an elegant pomaded young man behind the reception desk at the end of the lobby, and a woman in a blond mink coat who emerged from one of the boudoir-like recesses and gave me a quick glance of routine curiosity as I approached the desk. I gave her my own routine glance and, without thinking about it, classified her as slightly over-age, rich, good-looking, idle, and probably available to any interested, clean, adequately built, vigorous, and preferably inventive male.

I asked the pomaded young man for Mrs. Bellen.

"I am Mrs. Bellen," said the woman. "Are you Mr. Taliaferro?"

She was small, neatly made, and might have been taken for thirty-five by any passer-by, or forty by most people of her own class familiar with preservative devices, but she was probably recognisable as an easy forty-five by trained cosmeticians, There was nothing wrong with her face. She had large eyes of a light, impure blue, widely spaced, and nicely modelled cheekbones with small hollows beneath them—perhaps a shade too deep, these hollows. A shortish, straight nose. Mouth just a little strained, but expertly painted in an arresting off-geranium colour. She exuded a delicious scent, in discreet little whiffs, very light and flowery, just enough to suggest that you lean forward and smell more. Her hair was dark blonde, frankly touched up here and there, cut shortish with every hair in place, and she wore a small concoction of a hat in which fantasy struggled in a losing compromise with discipline. She could have been nothing in the world but an American. It was impossible to be sure, without preliminary by-play, whether she was a respectable wealthy suburban matron or a wealthy suburban whore.

"How awfully nice of you to look me up," she said. "I had no idea you really would."

"Why not?"

"Why should you?"

"Well..."

"Let's sit down."

She moved towards one of the recesses and I followed her. Her carriage was easy and straight. There was no tottering on the exaggeratedly high heels. Her ankles were a delight, and above them a pair of perfectly shaped but somehow rather hard-looking legs disappeared into shadowy mink caresses. She paused in front of a chair the colour of frozen champagne, upholstered in rose taffeta—and now I recognised the scent she used, rose, like field roses on a sunny day, and as long as I knew Audrey it was always roses, roses, roses.

She sat.

With some people, sitting is only a matter of shifting the area of support from the feet to the posterior without losing balance. With others it is a calculated act. With Mrs. Bellen it was straight out of ballet—graceful, easy, precise, smooth and alluring, terminating in a perfect attitude. She held it, smiling, while I lowered myself into the chair opposite her, then she relaxed a little and leaned back, throwing open her coat.

Now you can throw open a coat in a dozen different ways, and there is no reason why a coat shouldn't be thrown open in a warm room when you are fully dressed underneath it, yet Mrs. Bellen managed to make the throwing open of her coat an exposure. All she exposed was a black suit that nipped in at the waist and then flared out again. It was like a hundred other suits you might see on any fashionable street except that you could tell this one cost as much as most of the others put together. The suit really nipped in; she had a good waist and above it plenty of evidence—possibly perjured—of good breasts. She crossed her legs, knowing exactly how they looked from any angle, proffering a foot for examination. Her feet were small and as beautifully made as the ankles, and enclosed, if you can call it that, in shoes composed of a high heel, an invisible sole, and about five straps per shoe—at, conservatively, somewhere around twenty dollars a strap. They had been designed on the premise that the wearer would never encounter any hazard of weather greater than one step from a taxi to a marqueed entrance, and that they would make any man aware of his own burliness. They did me. I felt taller and hairier.

Smiling, Mrs. Bellen said, "So you're Ellen's cousin."

"I don't know any Ellen. I'm a cousin of a friend of somebody who has a sister that knows you."

"Oh, dear! As bad as that! Such an imposition!"

"Ordinarily, yes. In this case, already a pleasure."

"Oh, well, thank you!" she said, with just enough exaggeration to make it a little mocking, and just enough extra smile to take the bite out of it. She had not obviously examined me, but I already had the feeling that I was classified in her book, and classified fairly accurately, as to income, physique, and availability for general use if the occasion should arise for me to be used.

I said, "The idea seems to be that I am supposed to show you Paris. But I get the impression you don't really need much help."

"Well, we have been here some time, and we do have friends," she said, almost as if in apology. "But it doesn't make you any the less nice for bothering."

"Let's do something anyway."

"Why, of course. I'd love to. When?"

"Lunch?"

"Oh, I can't. I'm tied up for lunch."

"Dinner?"

Then she gave me the first real surprise. So far she had been pleasant enough and all, but fairly true to type. She said matter-of-factly, "I'm a little old for you," as she might have matter-of-factly stuck a hatpin through her cheeks.

She looked at me speculatively, reached some kind of decision, and went on, "—and anyway I'm tied up for the evening too. I just can't get out of it. I'd love to, but I just can't. You know, I'm going to suggest something. I hope you won't mind. Just feel free to refuse this, if you want to. Will you? Refuse if you want to, I mean."

"Yes. I'm a good refuser."

She stopped and looked at me questioningly, but not very questioningly, I thought. Pretty assured.

"Ask," I said.

"You know, you're really quite engaging, Mr. Taliaferro," said Mrs. Bellen. She paused for one more smile and then got down to business. "It's about my daughter. We have tickets for *Les Indes Galantes* and—have you seen it?"

"No, I haven't. I want to." It was new just then, and tickets were next to impossible to get.

"Well how very convenient! And then I stupidly confused my appointments and have this one that I simply can't get out of, but I do want Marie Louise to go, and the poor child can't go alone. My daughter, that is."

I can't say exactly why I thought she was lying, but I was certain that she hadn't until that moment decided to confuse some appointments. I was being used, on the spur of the moment, and by an expert.

"Still a pleasure," I said.

"But that's perfect! Really, I think it's simply too—ah—fortuitous. Oh!—" shifting into a pretty expression of vexation—"but the tickets are in a dress section."

"That's all right. I may not look it, but I own a tuxedo."

"Silly! I know that, Mr. Taliaferro! I was just letting you know."

"Excuse me. Look, perhaps we might include dinner before the show. All three of us. Are you tied up that early?"

"I'm afraid I am. But I'm sure Marie Louise would love it. Poor child, she must get so tired of me. And really—you don't mind my being frank?—perfectly frank, I mean. Do forgive me, but—really, there's' no reason you should be put to any expense. You see I'm taking advantage of being so much older than you—"

"I'm thirty-odd," I said.

"Really? You look so much younger." But she would have said the same if I'd claimed I was going on fourteen. "I'm forty even."

"No fooling! It should look that good on the rest of us, Mrs. Bellen."

"Well, thank you once more." But she seemed to withdraw a little, and continued, "So why don't you have dinner here at the hotel, just the two of you, and sign the check for me? It's a three-star restaurant. You don't mind my suggesting this?"

"Maybe a little. Not much. Anyway, I know a nice little no-star restaurant that might offer your daughter some variety. Let me do it that way."

"You're really very sweet. All right then, it's arranged. Shall we say you pick her up here at six-thirty? The curtain's early."

"All right. But there's one thing we're forgetting."

"What's that?"

"Miss Bellen."

"Marie Louise? How do you mean?"

"Maybe she'd like to invite someone she knows better."

"Oh, I'll see to that," said Mrs. Bellen and, catching herself too late, changed it to, "Rather, I'm sure she'll be happy with the arrangement."

"You are? Just why?" The atmosphere had been a little creamy from time to time, but that chilled it.

She didn't answer immediately, but instead rose to her feet, with all the care and effectiveness she had used in sitting down, and as I stood up she started walking slowly back towards the desk and the elevator, with me at her side. She was trying to decide whether to rebuke my impertinence, I decided, as a middle-aged woman should have done, or to treat it as persiflage, as a young girl would have been free to do. She ended by ignoring my question, and after a few steps she said, as if we had not been skirting an excessive familiarity, "You know, Mr. Taliaferro, I want to be certain you realise how very obliging you are being. I do appreciate it. You must get awfully tired of having to look up friends of friends."

"I do, Mrs. Bellen. But I mean it when I say this is different."

She stopped walking now, and, standing stock still, while I waited, she glanced towards the desk, as if to guess whether the clerk could hear or not, decided he couldn't, and said to me in a very low voice, standing close to me, her face turned up, "I—I don't know whether I should mention it. But—you might find Marie Louise a little—a little bit, how shall I say it?— a little bit odd in manner."

I felt a premonitory chill. Standing as close together as we were, I could feel her breath as she spoke, trying to tell me that her daughter was crazy.

"Odd? How?"

"There! I knew it! Why did I have to go and say that? You sound all scared and suspicious. Just forget I said anything. After all—" and she stopped helplessly, or as if helplessly, which is not the same thing at all.

I didn't accept this invitation to say something, but stood waiting, and finally she said, "I shouldn't have said that. Probably you wouldn't have noticed anything at all. Everyone's so crazy nowadays anyway. It's just that Marie Louise has been under a—considerable emotional strain lately, and she isn't always quite—oh, dear! Now you'll be looking for it! And probably there won't be anything at all. There usually isn't. Let's forget it, shall we?"

"Anything you say."

She smiled, and took my arm. We began walking again. Some women take your arm, and that's that. Mrs. Bellen made it something special. No suggestive pressure, nothing obvious, but somehow saying, "This is my hand, on your arm. How very pleasant," without saying or doing anything you could place. She didn't mention Marie Louise again, didn't say anything, in fact, until we had reached the elevator. As I opened the door for her she said, "I've forgotten your name. Your first name, I mean."

"Hooper. People call me Hoop, of course."

"I'm Audrey, Hoop."

She was in the elevator now, and I closed the door, a wrought-iron thing of spirals and little flowers, so that I looked at her through a kind of black art-nouveau garden. Very effective. She said, with a dulcet but ambiguous suggestion of promise, "Good-bye, Hoop," and as the elevator started up, she raised one hand and wiggled the fingers at me. It was the first thing she had done which was a little too coy for her apparent age, but as the elevator disappeared I smelled the perfume, just a whiff floating down, just a couple of dollars' worth, and I admitted to myself that she had left me wanting to see her again.

Just to see what would happen.

"Plenty," I thought, "if you were fool enough to let it."

So much for Audrey.

Big liar.

In connection with something I will next get around to explaining, I stopped at the desk and asked the pomaded young man if he was expecting a Dr. Mary Finney and a Miss Emily Collins, from the Belgian Congo. He had been perfectly polite until then, but now his manner changed quickly to one of genuine respect. With Mrs. Bellen I was just another American, not as well dressed as the rest of the clientele. In connection with Dr. Finney and Miss Collins, I was suddenly connected with the Sûreté. Yes indeed, there were reservations for the two ladies. They were expected that afternoon.

I left my card, although I was expecting to meet their plane in a few hours. The letter from Africa had caught me just in time.

CHAPTER TWO

MARY FINNEY'S LETTER was direct and at least partially to the point:

> DEAR HOOPY:
> *Summarising that leprosy research in a paper for Paris, London, Edinburgh. Paris first. How about meeting Sabena flight 482 on the 10th? Emmy along too. She has turned into a nuisance, won't let me wear my sun helmet this trip, says I have to have a hat. Well, I have. God help us all.*
> *Love,*
> M. F., M.D.

Emmy had added her own postscript, in a hand as neat and wispy as Emmy herself: HOOPY DEAR, *so eager to see you again. How long has it been? Too long. Time is having its way with me; my weight is down to 94, alas, but Mary is as fine as ever. We love you, Hoopy, and are going to bother you terribly to show us Paris between Mary's engagements. These are terrible, there are so many of them. It makes me feel very important, but not Mary. Love,* E. COLLINS. *Oh—we will be at a hotel called the Prince du Royaume, and we are guests of the Sûreté, which impresses me. I am told it is very grand.*

I was a little impressed myself, to find myself moving in both of the two circles which frequented the Prince du Royaume—official guests and rich Americans.

So I went out to meet Mary Finney's plane. Even from a distance, behind the barrier where I had to wait while the passengers disembarked, there was no mistaking my pair of beauties. Mary Finney and Emily Collins could never have been much of a size, even as young girls, and time had exaggerated the difference. Where Dr. Finney had expanded Emmy Collins had contracted until now, even concealed within a winter coat, she looked like a bundle of dried twigs tied up with a string.

Dr. Finney is not a fat woman, but without question she is outsize. That morning she was not at home in her clothes. They were completely undistinguished, managing to suggest the truth, which was that they had been picked up in some Congo department store at the last minute by a woman who over a long period of time had been wearing slight variations on her routine working garb without regard for fashion, or for anything but comfort and practicality. Her hat sat on her head with the uncertain and temporary look of a hat placed on a statue. In the shoe department neither Dr. Finney nor Miss Collins had made any concession at all: both of them wore sturdy brogue-like affairs which were going to be perfect protection against thorns, scorpions, poisonous serpents, and other natural enemies encountered in Paris in February.

As they approached I saw that Emily had brightened her costume with an unconvincing white cloth gardenia on one lapel. Mary Finney was similarly embellished by a plump gold watch on a chain pinned over one hillock. Even from a considerable distance I could see that the good doctor's handsome freckles were unmuted by cosmetics of any kind, but Emily's grainy little face was dabbed with white talcum, generously applied as it might have been to a baby, to freshen and soothe rather than to beautify. None of these little artifices had done much to increase the pair's resemblance to Garbo and Grable or other classical types, but by the time they had crossed the intervening space I knew that, just as I had expected, here were the two most fascinating women in France.

Dr. Finney's expression was enigmatic or even severe, and I knew that she was concealing some inner agitation. Half a pace behind her, Emmy gave the impression of keeping her hand in that of an older, wiser protector's, walking in her usual relationship of four steps to each of Dr. Finney's three, but always managing to come out even at the proper interval, like one of those difficult passages in Chopin where the right and left hands are called on to do this same kind of thing. From time to time Dr. Finney would crane her neck to scan the clot of people in which I stood, but as they gained the enclosure they were intercepted by a trio of Frenchmen in morning coats and striped trousers. Dr. Finney regarded them with the friendly trust she might have placed in a trio of procurers, and her expression did not change a great deal even when she was presented with a scroll tied in tricoloured ribbon, to a peppering of flash-bulbs. Something went wrong and one of the photographers asked for a repeat. Dr. Finney handed back the scroll and she and the leading Frenchman each took an end of it, looking a little too much as if they were contesting it, I thought, while the bulbs flashed again. For a moment just after that, Dr. Finney's eyes met mine directly. I smiled, and could almost have started forward towards her. She gave me a look of happy recognition and then dropped the idea, just as I had, and the five of them, Dr. Finney and Miss Collins and the three Frenchmen, went on down the long corridor and left it free for the ordinary passengers to file in.

"All that damn foolishness at the airport," Dr. Finney called it an hour later, when I was sitting with her and Emily in the living-room of their suite at the Prince du Royaume. "I thought it would sure look bad to those Frenchmen if the first thing I did in Paris was accost a young man. Gosh," she said, leaning back in her chair and looking around the room, up at the crystal chandelier and all around at the walls with their pale, elegant panelling. "Is this usual in Paris? Makes me feel like a hick."

"Oh, dear, closed Tuesdays," murmured Emily, seated near-by at an effeminate little escritoire with a notebook and a Guide Michelin and pencil. "I've got us down for the Louvre Tuesday and it says here closed Tuesdays." She had a couple of pages ruled off into blocks, and now she began to erase what she had written in one of them.

"Thursday," murmured Dr. Finney, pulling it out of the air.

"We can't do it Thursday. We've got the Ministry of National Health, you know, Mr. What's-his-name."

"All day?"

"Goodness no, just the morning. Then lunch with the Belgian Ambassador. Then in the afternoon the reception at the Institute for Tropical Medicine. It's quite a day. Dinner with the Minister of Colonies. No, Mary, Thursday's impossible."

"When's that policeman's ball?" Dr. Finney asked.

"Wednesday," said Emily, checking it against her diagram. She saw my face and said, "Not really a policeman's ball, Hoopy. It's a dinner. And not really policemen, but detectives. The Sûreté. Mary's going to make this talk—this address."

Dr. Finney hitched uncomfortably in her chair and made grumbling noises from which the general sense emerged that she had been called up here by what she termed in a friendly enough way the goddamn Ministry of Colonies, to talk about tropical medicine and summarise her conclusions regarding the control of dysentery and leprosy in the back country and everybody else had jumped on her and taken advantage of what she called her innocence and good nature, and even the cops had sewed her up and got her to accept an invitation to dinner and then told her it was a dinner for her and that she was expected to give them an address, just because she had incidentally in the course of her activities solved a couple of murders on her own strictly amateur and personal basis and they had turned out to be fairly well known in the case books. But she would be, she muttered, goddamned if she knew what to say in the address. Everybody knew about those old cases of hers, they were old stuff.

"Solve a murder for them," suggested Emily. "A new one." Dr. Finney emitted a sound expressive of contempt and rejection best described as a snort, but Emily went on, "There must be a lot of unsolved murders in a city as big as Paris. You could just pick one out and read up on it, and solve it. There might even be one that's giving them a lot of trouble right now. Don't you see?"

There was no logical response to be made to this proposition, since it was offered in good faith, so I dropped back a few sentences and said to Emily, "I hope you have my name down in a couple of those squares."

"As a matter of fact, I have," said Emily. "I had you down for the Louvre, since you know pictures and all. Do you know architecture too?"

"Somewhat."

"Then we'll take the Ecclesiastical Architecture tour on Tuesday instead," she decided. "I thought we could take a little walk and see the major monuments in chronological sequence." I heard myself breathing heavily, but she went on undisturbed, checking against another list, "According to the guide-books the oldest remains are still incorporated in St. Julien-le-Pauvre. Romanesque. I thought we could start there and then go on to Notre Dame and work up through St. Séverin, and then maybe St. Eustache because of the Renaissance modifications and then into the Renaissance itself, St. Sulpice, for instance—"

"How far do you want to go with this?" I asked. "I can take off all day Tuesday. I'm my own boss."

"So can we, all day. It's our day off. We're having dinner Monday night with the Portuguese Legation, Angola and Cabinda you see, and something afterwards, and I guess they think by then we'll need to rest up. So we could do Middle Ages and Renaissance in the morning, and in the afternoon we could see any of several eighteenth-century churches and then I thought maybe Notre Dame de Raincy, the concrete one, for the twentieth century—maybe."

"You don't need a guide," I said, at almost the same instant that Dr. Finney said, "Emmy'll kill you. She's been trying to get me to climb the Eiffel Tower. When it has elevators."

"Rather famous elevators, as a matter of fact," Emmy said. "Installed the year I was born. But to get the real feeling, I think you should climb. Do you know," she recited, "that the Eiffel Tower is so light that its supports exert less pressure on the earth, per square inch, than Mary's exerting at this moment? Less downward pressure per square inch than the average man sitting in a chair, the book says. And Mary's bigger than the average man."

"Maybe I am, but you could have made it less wounding by choosing Hoop as your reference. It's obvious that you'd never hold the thing to its moorings in the gentlest breeze."

Emily responded promptly, "The oscillation at the summit is only six inches in the highest winds, and the height varies eight inches according to temperature."

I remembered that I had something special to offer even a guide-book exhauster like Emily. "I have an archaeologist friend who's doing some excavations of earlier stuff than St. Julien-le-Pauvre. Not even in the guide-books yet. In the basement of a night-club. It's the membership kind of thing, and I belong—The Flea Club."

"Improbable sounding spot for ecclesiastical remains," Dr. Finney commented, and Emmy said, "I've never been in a night-club, not even in the morning. We'll have to start there, right after breakfast."

I told them a little bit about The Flea Club, we made an appointment for eight o'clock the next morning, and I hurried home to put on my dinner jacket and then hurried back to the Prince du Royaume to pick up Marie Louise Bellen. It was getting to be quite a shuttle.

CHAPTER THREE

WHATEVER ITS NAME suggests, The Flea Club was no scrimey little dive. It was a semi-public night-club with a private section for members. I first went there one night with an American named Freddy Fayerweather, who collected modern painting and had come to be an acquaintance of mine through my gallery, where he would now and then buy a picture. The Flea Club was a spectator's paradise, and when Freddy said he would put me up for membership I said for him to go ahead and do it.

After the murder, there was a lot of wild yellow journalistic fabrication about The Flea Club and the goings-on there, but actually the place was fairly mild. Plenty of the members were wacky but plenty of the people who frequent any place that operates well into the night, either publicly or privately, are wacky. I enjoyed The Flea Club and even felt an affection for many of its regulars. And I liked to hear Nicole sing.

That's all I could answer when people asked me how it happened that somebody as un-Flea Club as I seemed to be spent so much time there.

The Flea Club hadn't been its real name originally. Originally it was called the Club Ste. Geneviève de Fli, since it was on the site of a church—a chapel, rather—by that name, which was thought of as a legendary structure until my archaeologist friend, Professor Johnson, got around to digging and discovered foundations indicating that it really had been there. The chapel was built between 800 and 850, and during the next 1100 years various things happened to it. It was small and easy to lose in a growing city. The level of Paris grew around it until the chapel floor was filled in to meet it. Finally what remained above ground, the upper half, was chopped off and something else was built on the spot. Building followed building, until at some time or other the space was dug out again where the interior of the chapel had been, and the stumps of the original columns, still in place, were incorporated with later masonry, in what had now become the cellar of the buildings that succeeded one another above it. By the time Professor Johnson appeared, there was a mid-nineteenth-century building of no particular distinction standing there, and the part of the cellar with the remains of the chapel incorporated in it had become the members' room of The Flea Club. It does seem a complicated and round-about way to build a *boîte de nuit.*

The cellar held a small bar, a piano, no stage, a few square feet of dance floor—I never saw anybody dance there, but it was a useful area—and enough room left over to crowd in tables and chairs for maybe as many as forty people at a time, if they were careful not to take deep breaths simultaneously, which would have crushed the more fragile members to death. To one side there was also a small, comfortable room containing a bed, a table, a lamp, a radio, and a bookshelf. This room was occasionally occupied overnight by a member in a pinch. The night before the murder, such a pinch developed.

The members' cellar could be entered through a door at half level from the back street, which was quiet and private, with the blank wall of the butt-end of another building taking up the entire area across from it. You could also enter or leave this cellar by a stairway and locked door, to which only members held keys, into the semi-public part of the club, on the ground floor, which was operated for income. Up here the bar was bigger and the décor was fancier—or, more accurately, there was an effort at décor, whereas the cellar was just whitewashed walls. You entered this semi-public part from the boulevard. Anyone could spend money there, with an introduction from a member, but you could bring only one guest at a time into the members' cellar. The upstairs bar was larger and the tables were a little roomier. It was a drink-and-listen place. The drinks were satisfactory, and Nicole was worth listening to.

Nicole's real name was Marguerite Bontemps, a solid honest name good enough for anybody, but she used Nicole—nothing else, just Nicole—to sing under. I've never liked these one-name professional names. I liked Nicole herself, though, in spite of several other things. For instance, in spite of the way she fixed herself up to look like a second-rate Dietrich when she could have been a first-rate Marguerite Bontemps. She had a wide-hipped, full-breasted peasant figure and one of those round straightforward faces that can be so engaging without being either beautiful or distinguished. The songs she did best, the ones she was beginning to be known for, were songs of the little people on the streets, in the best French music-hall tradition—the shop girl whose world is transformed by love, the old 'My Man' theme, and all the others, the kind of thing that can be nauseously cloying or really touching, depending on the singer.

I always told Nicole that she ought to drop the lamé gowns and the rhinestone bracelets and the blondined hair and the shaved-off and repainted eyebrows and the blue eye shadow and try being Marguerite Bontemps. But she was afraid to change. She was beginning to make a reputation as Nicole and besides, she said, whoever heard of a night-club singer who didn't look the part? Which I said was exactly the point.

She never said so, but perhaps she didn't like remembering Marguerite Bontemps. She was born on a farm, a real peasant. At the beginning of the war she had run off and come to Paris, not because of the war, not for fear of the Germans, although the farm was in Alsace, not too far from the border, but because the city offered her two things she had discovered she was going to need within the next several months—anonymity, and a charity ward. She kept body and soul together one way or another, largely by kitchen work and other domestic employment, and later on as a waitress. The baby was born six months after her arrival in Paris. She must have had a terrible struggle but she managed to support herself and care for the baby by various desperate stratagems until nearly the end of the war, when things began to pick up for her personally in spite of the toughness of the general situation, and she was able to place the child in a convent home near Grenoble, where it still was when I knew her.

She began to sing almost by accident. Like so many Alsatians she spoke as much German as French, and during the Occupation she began making her own doggerel translations of popular songs of the Piaf type, singing them literally on street corners. She had always enjoyed singing, imitating Piaf and other popular favourites from gramophone records. Her voice had a harsh quality when she forced the high notes of her small range, and almost a guttural quality on the lower ones, although it was of extraordinary sweetness and warmth in between. Now she suddenly discovered that these natural defects gave a piquancy to her singing that a conventionally better voice would never have had.

She had a bad experience at this time. She said that it never occurred to her that singing for Germans' tips was any worse than waiting at tables for them, but one afternoon she was pretty badly knocked about by three women who might have done her real harm if the police hadn't intervened. She never sang in German again, but she had discovered her voice, and she worked from that time on towards a single goal—to be a singer and make a living at it. She was not at first ambitious for a name and she didn't even consider the possibility that she might make really big money. She set about capitalising on her voice as she might have set about investing a small unexpected inheritance. She had a little something and she intended to make maximum use of it within the limits of safety.

Nicole never at any time had a great stroke of luck. She had no rich sponsor. She sang anywhere, under any conditions, for any money she could get, accumulating a reputation with a tenacity and a single-mindedness almost obsessive. She worked in her profession with exactly the same acceptance of long hours and hard work and exactly the same recognition of the importance of every small profit that she would have expected if she had been opening a shop. She was astute, she was intensely practical, and as a singer she was increasingly sensitive. In her middle thirties, at The Flea Club, she was coming into her own.

She was not only the singer at The Flea Club, she was also its general manager for the members. She kept the books, which nobody ever bothered to look at, did what buying was necessary, handled the cash, and supervised the staff, which was small. Her crutch and her support and her Rock of Gibraltar was an old woman we knew only as Bijou, who was part personal maid and part housekeeper. Nicole's life seemed as steady, as open, as industrious, and as well regulated as you could ask. It was, if anything, lacking in variety and excitement.

This was the woman that Mary Finney, Emily Collins, Professor Johnson and I were to discover, with her head bashed in, half buried in one of the pits of Professor Johnson's excavations in the basement of The Flea Club, on the morning of the day which we had expected to consume by Emmy's chronological tour of ecclesiastical architecture and architectural remains in Paris.

CHAPTER FOUR

IT HAD BEEN a Saturday morning when I met Audrey Bellen for the first time, and it was the same afternoon when Mary Finney and Emily Collins came in on the plane. So much I have already set down in this account. It was on the Tuesday morning following that we found Nicole. A lot happened in between, which I can't really be blamed for not having recognised at the time as events which were to culminate in a murder. Now, in my apartment back of the gallery, with her feet propped up on another chair ("Excuse the vulgarity, Hoop, but I always think better this way") Mary Finney sat ruminating out loud. The police had taken over The Flea Club; the four of us had answered what questions they had thought necessary for the time being; we had had lunch ("Go ahead and eat what's put before you, Hoop. I appreciate your spiritual distress and I know some people can't stand the sight of blood, but I've got an idea and I think you're going to need your strength.") and Emily Collins and

Professor Johnson had gone off together to try to crowd post-Flea Club Ecclesiastical Architecture into what remained of the day. I was making coffee on my alcohol lamp. One thing I'll say for myself: I make good coffee. I had been telling Dr. Finney about Nicole—where she came from, what her career had been, and so on—all the things I have just set down here.

"You've been a member of this Flea Club thing for some time, haven't you, Hoopy?"

"Eight months or so."

"You know the people around here. The ones that knew this Nicole best."

"I don't know anyone who'd want to kill her."

"That's what I'm getting at. How do you know you don't know anyone who'd want to kill her?"

"I don't know anyone that I can *imagine* would want to kill her for any reason whatso—"

"That's an altogether different matter. Depends on the quality of your imagination. Also, you're too close to it. Now me—I'm not close to it at all."

"That's right."

"And my imagination runs towards suspicion. Emmy thinks it's awful, but there it is. You, Hoop—you're sort of a trusting, think-the-best-of-people, innocent-type boy."

"Well, thanks."

"I hadn't thought of it as a compliment. Now what I want you to do, I want you to tell me all about everybody."

"You want me to—I wouldn't know where to begin!"

"Yes you would. Think of The Flea Club for a minute. Go ahead, visualise it." I went ahead and visualised it. "Now just name somebody, anybody."

"Audrey." It just popped out.

"See?" Dr. Finney said, "We've already started."

"Would you mind," I said, and whatever she thought about the quality of my imagination, I was getting suspicious, "telling me where we're going?"

"I'm going to get my talk together for this police banquet thing. Now wait a minute," she said, putting up her hand as I started to protest. "I realise this has to be a purely artificial kind of thing, but it's going to be an exercise in method and then I'll expound it with my conclusions to these French cops. I haven't got any idea I'll be lucky enough to catch a murderer—"

"Oh, yes you have."

She gave me a really nice grin.

"What is this method that I'm going to need my strength for, to give you an exercise in?" I asked.

She settled herself into the chair, taking on a look of permanence like some great natural monument. "Well, it goes like this. Somebody gets knocked on the head. Somebody else, obviously, did it. Everybody's surprised. Now, murder always happens for a big reason. At least it's big to the people involved. All of a sudden it happens, and part of the shock is that you realise it hasn't actually come out of a clear sky, something's been going on for a long while—"

"Not necessarily such a long—"

"—in the lives of at least two people, murderer and murderee, that you haven't even suspected. Fingerprints and all that stuff I don't know anything about. But what I figure is, if you examine the lives of the people all around the victim you find some things in their lives that don't explain themselves. And in the victim's life too. Now if you can invent an explanation that fills all the holes, it might be the true one. You invent explanations no matter how unsupported they may seem to be except by one little inconsistency in that person's life, and if the same explanation explains away the inconsistencies in another's, then maybe you're getting things to dovetail. See?"

"I guess so. I don't know how comfortable it makes me feel around you, though. We've all got inconsistencies."

"I take it for granted you didn't knock Nicole on the head," Dr. Finney said graciously, "and I say again this is just an abstract exercise. We've only got a few hours—just this afternoon and tonight—so we'll arbitrarily limit the characters to those around The Flea Club. You ready to begin telling me about this Audrey person?"

"Where do I begin?"

"What's her connection with The Flea Club, for instance? A member?"

"No. She turns out to be all tied up with somebody I know who is a member."

"All right. Tell me about her. From the beginning."

So I told her about the letter from my cousin in Madison, and how I went around to the Prince du Royaume, and how Audrey was already there in the lobby, and how we sat in one of the rose-quartz side rooms, and how Audrey was dressed, and what we said, and how she smelt, and how she finagled me into a date with Marie Louise to see *Les Indes*, and what my impressions were in general. I kept strictly to what had happened that morning without anything that came later, just as I have already set it down here.

Dr. Finney leaned way back in her chair during the whole telling, her eyes on the ceiling, not saying a word, and when I would pause and look at her she would gesture 'go on,' right up until I came to the end, seeing Audrey off in the elevator, and getting the last whiff of field roses, and wondering what would happen with Audrey if you were fool enough to let it.

I stopped, and Dr. Finney remained immobile in her chair, by now in a position which you would have to call sprawled. Her reddish, freckled face was blank, as it always was when special things were going on behind it, and as I looked I compared her with Audrey Bellen, not to Audrey's advantage, and when she spoke I discovered that she had been making the same comparison, but in a different direction.

"These damn pretty women," she said suddenly, and sat up. "Especially these damn pretty women who stay pretty for ever. You know, Hoops, I was quite a bouncing corn-fed girl myself, back in Kansas, and there were even a couple of young fellows I probably should've taken up in their weakness, but I had this doctoring bug. Tell me—d'you think Audrey enjoys life? She have any fun?"

"No, not really. I've a lot more to tell you about her. How do you want the rest of it—everything about Audrey now, or everybody all mixed up?"

"Mixed up, sort of. I've got a working sketch of Audrey. Play her against somebody else."

"Marie Louise?"

"The crazy pregnant daughter. Yes."

I tried to make my own face blank, because I knew something I wanted to hide from Mary Finney, something special about Marie Louise. I happened to know that Marie Louise had been in The Flea Club that morning, only a few hours ago, when Dr. Finney and Emmy and Professor Johnson and I had discovered Nicole, and that she had been there all night, and that I had got her out of there.

"I don't know whether it's worth while spending your time telling you about Marie Louise. She's not a Flea Club member in the first place—"

"Nor is Audrey."

"No."

"Well, then."

"But Marie Louise—I mean she couldn't have had anything to do with it, it's absurd on the face of it, a sweet girl like that, so why waste time? If she's obviously not the kind of girl who—well—"

I stopped from sheer loss of momentum, dragged down by guilty conscience. Dr. Finney looked at me with suspicion and then certainty. "Well I'll be damned," she said deliberately, but not with irritation. "Hiding something! Do you know what a nice wide-open pan you've got? Well, all in good time."

She sighed heavily. "Let's make some more coffee on that thing," she said, "and you tell me about Marie Louise." We both got up and went over to the table and started fussing around. I went to the bathroom to get some tap water, still thinking about Marie Louise, and I heard Mary Finney call from the other room, asking, "Slept with her yet?"

"*What!*" I yelled, outraged. "*Certainly not!*"

"Well, you needn't be so vehement," said Dr. Finney mildly. "People do."

I came back into the room, saying huffily, "She's a nice girl." Dr. Finney had the lamp going. It looked cheery, and Dr. Finney herself was so calm and homely that I decided I didn't mind what she asked me.

"As a matter of fact I wasn't thinking of Marie Louise," she said. "I was thinking of Audrey."

"I don't think it's any of your business."

"You might be right. Unless it could have to do with the question at hand. And who knows, it might. So I might be asking you again. And if I do, don't shout. And don't swear. It's unbecoming in a young man. Now tell me about Marie Louise."

And so while we made the coffee, and then while we went back and sat down and drank it, I told her about the first time I saw Marie Louise.

I certainly can make good coffee. I admit it. Even on an old beat-up alcohol lamp.

I had changed my mind so many times about Marie Louise during the past three days, and she had given me such a shock that very morning, that when I had to tell Mary Finney about her, I had trouble sticking to exactly the impression she had made on me when she first came down into the lobby that Saturday night. I don't know whether you'd have turned to look at Marie Louise if she had passed you on the street. Depends on what you want in a girl, and how quick your eye is. There was nothing exceptional about her at all, except that everything about her was right. Her hair was neither dark nor light, but somewhere in the vast middle register where most hair must be classified. It was thick and glossy, cut medium long-short, parted on one side and brushed back from her face. Her eyes were a grey-blue, with lashes a little darker than you would have expected. She had a nose-shaped nose without any particularly individual protrusions or declivities, and a sweet soft mouth which might or might not remain sweet and soft as she grew older. She seemed to be about seventeen or eighteen. Her skin was fresh and clear, and except for the usual brilliant lipstick, of which I certainly approve, she used a minimum of make-up. Probably none. She didn't need it. As a matter of fact, she was an awfully pretty girl, but you were likely to miss it because she didn't act like one.

She came across the lobby in a mink coat nearly as luxurious as Audrey's, open so that I saw a soft blue-grey dress of some kind which revealed everything while it exposed nothing. She had a lovely figure and nothing short of a barrel could have hidden it entirely. She walked beautifully, not the way Audrey walked, not with the calculation and artifice and suggestion of a mannequin, but with exactly the easiness and the natural grace that Audrey had lost for ever. She didn't know she was walking one way or another. She just walked to get from one spot to another, and it was good.

As I stood up she gave me a quick appraising glance that I thought held a certain amount of relief.

"Hello," she said.

There's no way to write it the way she said it. It was damn near rude. Not with intention, but because her complete indifference was apparent in the two syllables, behind their casualness. She wasn't interested in me, she wasn't interested in *Les Indes Galantes*, and she wasn't interested in dinner. If she was interested in anything, it was in getting back to the hotel which we hadn't even left yet. This is a bad thing in a young girl. And as she came closer I saw that she had been crying. She had been crying hard and crying for a long time.

"Mama's upstairs," she said impersonally. "She says to ask you would you like to come up for a drink ?" Her voice was soft and low, pleasant, but with the air of fatigue that I could see now around her eyes. I thought 'mama' was just about the most inappropriate word in the world for Audrey.

"How about you?" I asked. "Would you like one?"

"I don't drink," she said indifferently, and stopped, as if we could have stood there just as we were, for the next four hours, and she would have remained perfectly passive, not caring whether I said anything or whether we did anything. She was marking time, that's all, and it wasn't any more difficult to mark time with me than to mark it some other way. It was all the same to her.

"Then we'll go on to the restaurant and I'll have something while we wait," I said.

"All right."

Without being a Don Juan, I have always had at least normal success with women, and once or twice I have surprised myself. But I was certainly a failure that night. I just couldn't make any time at all. It wasn't a game. I wasn't on the make. All I wanted was to spend the time pleasantly. It was a restaurant I especially liked, but Marie Louise rose to the surface for one remark, one volunteered remark. "This is a nice little place," she said, and then lapsed back into indifference. "It's a *damn* nice little place," I told her, "and not to be condescended to." A little something flickered back of her eyes and she even gave the suggestion of a smile. "I didn't mean to condescend," she said. "I think it's a nice little place and I said so."

Les Indes is a tremendous ballet spectacle, with a shipwreck and a live volcano spouting real flames at one point. During a ballet of flowers, when the queen appears—she's a rose—the whole Opera is sprayed with rose perfume. (I thought of Audrey.) Marie Louise sat politely, no more stirred by everything that three centuries of French gimcrackery could work up for her entertainment than she was by her escort, which was some comfort to me. During the interval, when everybody strolls and gives everybody else the eye, I was proud to be with such a pretty girl, but if anybody tried to figure us out they must have thought either that we had had a lovers' quarrel or been married a little too long. Or maybe they just thought we were English. Anyway, they looked at Marie Louise with immediate approval, and then came that quick waning of interest that comes with the discovery that there's nothing stirring.

When the final curtain came down I said, "I know some of the ballerinas. Would you like to go backstage?" I don't know any ballerinas, but I knew I was safe. By this time I was playing all by myself. "No, I don't think so," Marie Louise said. "I guess I'd better go back home." "Home" made her think of something, and she changed it to "back to the hotel."

So we went back to the hotel, and that would have been that, and I'd never have seen her again, if I hadn't got mad. I have an MG, and most people enjoy riding in it, but Marie Louise took it for granted, and sat there lovely and indifferent as she was driven through the most beautiful city in the world, after seeing one of the most beautiful spectacles ever staged, in just about as engaging a little car as there is, with a perfectly acceptable man as chauffeur. I drove her up to the marquee of the hotel and almost stopped, and then I got mad. She was already leaning forward to get out when I gunned the little car so that it snapped her right back into her seat when it shot forward. I took it fast until I saw a vacant place at the kerb, then I jammed on the brakes and swerved in. I am not ordinarily a fancy driver but this was a good clean job.

I turned off the ignition and the lights and turned to Marie Louise and said, "Now listen, you. Goddamn it, come to life."

She looked at me with her face wide open and made a little sound like "ooooooo" and I said, "For God's sake, cry or scream or hit me or something," and she did. She burst into tears. Really burst into them, like something breaking. She wedged herself into the corner against the door as far as she could get from me and made all those terrible sounds people make when they cry out loud.

I sat, letting it go on and wear itself out. When she began to calm down she sounded a lot like the subsiding passages after the storm sequence in the *William Tell* Overture. Finally she partially disengaged herself from the corner, sat up a little straighter, managed to say "Oh, dear," gave a large hiccup, blew her nose hard, looked up at me, and smiled. It was wet and it was feeble and it seemed to call into play a set of muscles that had begun to atrophy from lack of use, and it faded out pretty quick, but it had been there, and it had been something that without question you could call a smile.

"Feel better?"

The smile came back. "I guess I do."

"Want to tell me about it?"

She shook her head. "Why should I? It couldn't possibly interest you," she said wearily enough.

"Why not?"

"You don't know me. I don't know you, either. It's all so silly and pointless, even trying to be polite or anything. Don't try to be sympathetic. Thanks all the same. May I get out now?"

"Just a minute. Look, I'm really getting curious. What is it? Love?"

She opened her eyes a little wider, in surprise, not that I had asked, but only that I even found it necessary to ask. "Why naturally!" she said. "Whatever else could anyone feel so bad about?" And then, "Now stop it. I don't want to talk about it. I want to go back to the hotel."

Ordinarily I don't believe in trying to pick up the scraps and patch them together, but Marie Louise looked prettier all the time. "Not the hotel," I said. "Let's give us another chance. Let's go somewhere."

"Oh, no. I couldn't."

"Yes, you could."

"I just couldn't."

"Ever hear of The Flea Club?"

"The what?"

"Flea Club."

"Goodness no. If I'd ever heard of anything called The Flea Club I'd have remembered it."

"Maybe I shouldn't take you there anyway. It's not a place for young girls." This was partly true, but only mildly, and was supposed to stir her up a little. Anyway, I wouldn't have taken her down into the cellar, where things really did get pretty relaxed sometimes, but only to the bar upstairs, where things were conventional, as bars go.

But she said, "I can't go anywhere at all. I just can't."

"You're leaving me with an awfully soggy impression."

"Soggy! Well I like that! I've never been called soggy before!"

"You've been soggy tonight, child."

"I'm afraid I have." She gave a final blow to her nose and said, "Well, I can't do anything about it now. Take me back. I've had a perfectly dreadful time but it isn't your fault. I want to go back to the hotel."

"Then that's that." I swung the car round and proceeded at normal speed back to the hotel. At the elevator I said to Marie Louise, "I'm sorry the evening was such a failure."

"You needn't feel bad about it," she said. "I was just awful, but I—oh, let's drop it. I'm sorry. Thanks anyway."

"You're welcome."

"Good night then."

"Good night."

And then I said, "Marie Louise, do you know you're pretty?"

For a moment I thought she was going to look pleased, but inexplicably her expression changed to one which, of all things, was more like contempt.

"Pretty? Me? Don't be silly."

"But you are. Everything about you is just right. You've got lovely hair and skin—" and I was going to go on and tell her the rest, including maybe that if only she would *act* like a pretty girl it would be noticeable that she *was* one, but she interrupted me with a voice that wasn't pretty at all.

"How much did she pay you to say that?" she asked.

"Pay me to—who?"

"Audrey. Who do you think?"

"I don't think anybody. I certainly don't think Audrey. And I sure as hell don't know exactly what you're aiming at."

"I'm aiming at not being taken in by anybody," Marie Louise said.

I could have got good and mad then, but I looked at her and saw a pretty girl with a profound distrust of her own attraction and I thought, 'Audrey, you unholy bitch,' but what I said to Marie Louise was, "Audrey didn't pay me anything or suggest that I say anything, with or without pay. If you want to know, she offered to pay the dinner check, which was within the bounds of acceptability under the circumstances although I didn't accept it. I took you out because I wanted to see *Les Indes Galantes* and when you walked into the lobby I thought it was going to be a good evening. I'm still ready to take you to The Flea Club."

"I don't want to go to The Flea Club," she said, "and I don't want ever to see you again. I'm sorry, and thanks, but this has been even worse than usual. Any time you want to see Audrey I'm sure she'll be glad to oblige. So good night."

"And a good, good night to you," I said, and shut her into the elevator and walked away. "And a great big hug for Audrey when she tucks you in," I thought, and then I decided that whatever went on between the two of them wasn't anything for me to worry about, and I set out for The Flea Club, because I had missed it during the past couple of weeks and because it was always one of the most restful places I knew. Although whenever I have said to other people that I found The Flea Club restful, they have always said that I was stark, raving mad.

I told all this to Mary Finney and waited for her comment.

"Apparently not pregnant," Dr. Finney said.

"Not in that dress."

"Crazy?"

"Just because a girl doesn't respond to me, it doesn't mean she's irrational."

"Odd, though. Pretty, rich, apparently healthy, attractive to men, which usually means attracted *to* men. Ought to have enough resilience to have recovered from any busted love match, at that age. She didn't like you at all? No response at all? Just nothing?"

"Just nothing. Of course I'm older than she is."

"Pooh," said Dr. Finney. "Girls that age are thrilled by that."

"I thought at first maybe she was manic-depressive and I'd hit her in the bottom of the cycle."

"Possible."

"No, it isn't. I've seen her since then, and she's all right."

"You have? How many times?"

"Couple."

"Don't tell me about it now," said Dr. Finney. "I want to hear about The Flea Club. You did go there? See any of the regulars?"

"Several of them."

"Good. Tell me about it. 'A Night at The Flea Club'."

"It's going to take a little while," I warned her hopefully. My voice was already beginning to feel the strain. "Don't you want a recess?"

"Oh, that's all right," said Dr. Finney considerately. "Don't mind me. Just go right ahead."

I went ahead.

CHAPTER FIVE

I INSIST THAT even the private cellar of The Flea Club was essentially a quiet and orderly place, dedicated to the principle of live and let live, and I have taken many a visitor down there who came out saying he could have found more excitement in the lounge of his local Y.M.C.A. A lot depended on the kind of night you hit. I have taken people there who had hinted they would love to go, and have looked upon me coldly afterwards and said there hadn't been a person in the place they would have admitted to their drawing-room back home. It is useless to point out to them that they hadn't been asking to be taken somewhere where they could find somebody to take back home to their drawing-room, and there you are, left with that uncomfortable feeling that there must be something wrong with you because you were a member and enjoyed being there.

I know half the members were monsters, but I didn't mind. I know exactly the kind of person Freddy Fayerweather was, but I enjoyed listening to his confidences. I didn't like René

Velerin-Pel too much, but he was decorative. Also I enjoyed making pools with myself as to the age and approximate fortune of the next woman René would show up with and as to how long it would be before it became obvious that she was giving him what he wanted from her—money. And so on. And if all that indicates anything unsavoury about me, why, fine.

On the night I've been talking about, when I took Marie Louise to *Les Indes*, we were followed to the Opera from the hotel. We were also followed back from the Opera. And after I had seen her to the elevator and had come back out, I was followed to The Flea Club. When I was recounting these events to Mary Finney, I didn't know about this. I mention it here to fill things in.

There was certainly no reason to suspect I might be followed. I hadn't done anything unusual or so far as I knew been involved in anything unusual anyone else was doing. I had gone to see an ageing clotheshorse friend of a friend, and had taken her daughter to the theatre. I had never seen either of them before and I never expected to see either of them again. I was only conscious that I had had a disastrous evening with a pretty young girl, disastrous to my ego at any rate, since it had become obvious that she would just as soon be skinned alive as prolong the evening in my company beyond the period contracted for. But my conscience was clear as a bell.

The first thing you saw when you came into The Flea Club by the boulevard entrance was likely to be Bibi. Bibi wasn't a member, but she had the run of the place. It's hard to say just what her position was. Certainly she was a great annoyance to Nicole, but the rest of us liked having her around. She was a kind of club mascot.

She came to the club nearly every night and took up her station at the end of the bar nearest the entrance, where she could keep her eye out for free drinks. It would be difficult to be more explicit as to her age than to say that she was under twenty. Prophecy was easy, though. In ten years she was going to look forty, if she lived. By definition, I'm afraid she was a prostitute, since her only source of income was the largesse of the various people she slept with, but the definition somehow doesn't fit. She was as soft and as wriggly and as affectionate as a pup. She wasn't educated at all, and she probably wasn't very bright. I doubt that it ever occurred to her that any question of right or wrong was involved in her life. She got hungry, she loved whisky, and she thought people were nice to be with. It was just the most fortunate thing in the world that they liked to give you things, drinks and dinners and such clothes as you needed (sweaters and skirts, it came down to) and, for all I know, she made only a tenuous connection between the pleasure and comfort of sharing somebody's bed and the little bit of money in the morning.

Sometimes I used to worry about Bibi, thinking that something ought to be done to straighten her out. But Nicole in her common-sense way would say, "Why? There is nothing in life for that little type. She is lucky to have what she is getting now. There is nothing to do for one like that."

And that was true. Bibi was a born stray. Certainly Nicole's origins were as humble, but in the gene lottery Nicole had come by a sustaining shrewdness, while Bibi was marked from the beginning for the sore eye, the mange, the vermin, and the ultimate dog-catcher.

"What should really be done," Nicole would say, "is to get rid of that little one now, before she becomes an embarrassment."

"But you can't do a thing like that to Bibi," I objected.

"Why not? One must be practical. It is bad for the club. For you others the club is only a place to amuse yourself. For me it is a living and a career. I don't like having Bibi around."

"She doesn't do any real harm."

"True. Not yet. I know it is all right just now. But some time she will make a terrible scandal, or worse. She is not a child of good sense. She picks up these visitors at the bar, she is very convenient for members who are lonesome for the night. All that I accept. That is the way things are. But she is not a child of good sense. Let us imagine that some day she steals the wallet of one of these pick-ups."

"Bibi never stole a thing in her life."

"She has never found it necessary. So far everyone gives her everything. But some time she will do something really foolish which requires real money to amend. At a place like this, everything is all right until someone makes a scandal to the police. Then it is finished."

But Bibi had already established herself as our pet. It was too late to drown her in a bucket of warm water, and none of us wanted the job of taking her out in the country and losing her. So we all patted her and played with her and enjoyed her cute ways.

She was at her station near the door when I came in, her face already a little blurry with whisky, and she stopped me with her broad-mouthed, sweet and meaningless little smile and said, "*Allô*, 'Oopee. You buy me a drink?"

"Hello, Bibi. No. You've already got a drink."

She also had a plump middle-aged pink-faced companion who looked at me belligerently. He needn't have worried. It was only an habitual proposition. Bibi knew three English phrases and she liked to use all three of them on me, in tribute. Bibi especially liked Americans. She kept on smiling, eager to go on with the rest of her repertoire. "Okay, meester," she said, which was number two, and then wound up to her finale: "You teekleesh?" She reached inside my coat and wiggled her fingers along my ribs. Her hand was like a baby rabbit in there.

"Not ticklish tonight. So long, Bibi," and as I left I heard the plump pink-faced man say hopefully, "I'm ticklish."

Across the room I caught a glimpse of René, his handsome face in my direction as he leaned forward towards his companion at the table, whose thin, expensive silhouette I recognised as his Mrs. Jones's, as usual, and I wondered how much per month, or per performance, René was hitting her for, while he looked round for his jackpot.

Most of us who followed René's affairs took it for granted that Mrs. Jones herself was being lined up as the jackpot.

God knows she was susceptible enough. She had already been married and divorced from four dyed-in-the-wool sons-of-bitches. There was a beautiful consistency about Mrs. Jones's marriages and affairs. A man had to be only two things, and she was overboard: he had to be handsome, and he had to be a son-of-a-bitch.

None of her four husbands had been named Jones, nor had she, and although she took the name Jones around the club, her identity could be no secret to anybody who had followed the tabloids during the past twenty-five years. She had been married, in order of appearance, to an Italian count, a Georgian prince, an English jockey, and an American prize fighter. They had all left their marks on her, each in his own fashion. The Italian count had taken a good healthy naïve rich bouncing ignorant American girl and had trained her in *couture* and *toilette*, reduced her weight by thirty pounds, and made her an international party-goer with an insatiable appetite for the bed. The Georgian prince had added a brief fling at heroin. The English jockey had given her a taste for gambling, and the American prize fighter a two-inch scar along her right temple. But she still had a good half of her original fortune left, thanks to the diligence of her lawyers and brokers, and she even had a suggestion of her original good looks, and it was hard to understand why René hadn't yet cabbaged on to these remainders via holy matrimony. She gave every sign of being ready, and it was time René settled down.

Near-by, Freddy Fayerweather was leaning across another table in very much the same eager manner that Mrs. Jones was leaning towards René, and opposite Freddy I recognised the neat flare-shouldered back of Nicole's accompanist, Tony Crew—changed from Croute for professional reasons, at Freddy's suggestion. For that matter, Freddy had changed his own name—not legally, yet, which he had to wait to go back to the States to do, but he used Fayerweather for everything except signing. His real name was Frederick all right, but his last name was Gratzhaufer. Frederick Gratzhaufer is quite a name, but it certainly doesn't suggest the sort of fluttering chappy that Freddy Fayerweather was.

"And I *do* think a person's name ought to sug*gest* them, don't you think?" Freddy said. "Imagine Tony and me—'Croute and Gratzhaufer.' So I say, why not? Why not change? Don't you think so? I mean I think it's im*per*ative, don't you? And there's this simply wonderful *build*ing at the University of Virginia—I'm a Virginia man, did you know? Yes, my dear, *three whole months*, three whole months of *ab*solute *hell*, then I simply couldn't bear it and left—but there's this Fayerweather Hall there, and at first I thought I'd take over the whole name, be Mr. Hall, you know, which isn't bad, really—Fayerweather Hall, Esquire. Nice? But then I do think there's something of the Freddy in me, much as I *hate* to admit it, so...Anyway, I think Crew is perfect for Tony, don't you? Tony Crew. *Just* like him. Antoine Croute—no. But Tony—well, he's really a *na*tural for that, and then Crew—you know, crew cuts, crew shirts, all that neat, lean muscled *mas*culine association. So I really think—" and then he would stop all this babbling, as he frequently did, by a phrase he was fond of using as a period. "Well, *any*way," he would say.

Tony Crew was one of the quietest people around The Flea Club and he tolerated Freddy with a patience anyone else would have been hard put to it to equal, since Freddy kept him continuously under assault. Tony was not only Nicole's accompanist, he also wrote some of her songs. I liked him, as everybody did. With his face and figure and natural attraction he could have gone into René's business and made a million, but nobody ever got very close to Tony. He was as quiet and retiring as Freddy was yappy and gregarious. For that matter, I liked Freddy all right too, but when I came to The Flea Club the night I'm telling about, I didn't feel like joining him and Tony because I didn't feel like talking to anybody who was always in quite as much of a dither about everything as Freddy always was. I looked around for Professor Johnson, who had turned into a regular as the unexpected result of his excavations in the cellar, but if he was around, he was downstairs, so I had a long quiet drink alone at the bar—alone meaning that I didn't know anybody there who was shouldering me, as the time for Nicole's next turn approached and the room began to fill up.

Tony got up and left to join Nicole; Freddy followed him out of the room with his eyes, and then, turning back, caught sight of me, and jumped up from his table and came blithering over.

"Hell*oooo*, Hoop!" he began babbling. "You're back! *How* was Italy? You *must* tell me all about it. But not now, not *now*! My dear, *what* you've missed!" Freddy's 'my dear' was for everybody. I once heard him use it on a cop who stopped him at an intersection, and there were a couple of difficult moments.

"*Such* goings on," he was saying now. "You've missed simply everything. You wouldn't believe! *Too* exciting! "

Talking was a compulsion with Freddy. I've seen him really try to stop, when he knew he was sounding like an ass, and I've seen him unable to dam up the torrent of prattle that kept coming out in spite of himself. "Why do I *do* it?" he once wailed to me. "Why can't I *help* it? I *know* how I sound." He spoke in a fairly high but not abnormally high voice, at approximately the speed of light, except that he would hit one in every ten or so syllables and accent it and draw it out so that his talk went forward in a series of lurches, further deformed by the honkings and squawkings of a fake British accent which had become second nature.

"Simply *ev*erything has happened," he chattered. "*Some*thing has happened to *every*body. Except *me*, of course. Nothing ever happens to *me*! Isn't it sad? Poor Freddy. But it doesn't, it simply doesn't. I can't understand it. Professor Johnson's found himself a new buttress. *Have* you been downstairs, Hoopy?"

"Nope."

"Well do go! I mean the place is simply fan*tas*tic, these utterly tremendous *holes*, right in the middle of the *clubroom*, and the most tre*men*dous piles of dirt. Really quite picturesque and too *too* archaeological! So intel*lect*ual, is the way I feel about it, so *un*-Flea Club! But good, you know, really good. The Institute's been taking pictures, if you can imagine. I mean it—the *In*stitute! Ninth century if it's a day, Professor Johnson says. Can you i*mag*ine?"

"Hot stuff," I said.

"*Is*n't it?" Freddy agreed enthusiastically. The syllables kept spilling out, and I stood watching him and wondering about him. When you first saw Freddy Fayerweather you thought he was a good-looking boy. Then as soon as he moved or opened his mouth, it was gone. He had a freshness of tint and a nice regularity of feature, with heavy straight glossy blond hair, cut a little long but always neatly combed and trimmed, and he had a naturally pleasant and masculine proportion as to general width and height which looked even better by the time his tailor dressed him. But he moved wrong. When he described himself as 'all cartilage and blubber' as against Tony's fine-boned tautly sinewed build, he was selling himself short but it was true that he had an over-flexible and slightly soft look. You might have taken him for anything from a second-string saxophone player to an Oxford undergraduate, if he had been dressed exactly like either one, but he was always tailored with that absolute perfection attainable only by the rich American imitating the well-dressed Britisher. In the matter of accessories, Freddy was passionate. Everything was impeccable, quiet, and incredibly expensive. He was the most fanatically clean-looking individual I've ever known, and the most juvenile in appearance for his age. He was probably around twenty-five, and if he lived another fifty years he was going to look like other septuagenarians of his type—like an adolescent prematurely withered by some corrosive ailment.

"—and René's got a new woman," he was saying. "And *has* he worked fast on this on! My dear, I'm sure he's already given her the free *sam*ple, and now she's simply sitting up and begging. Too too nymph over him, really. Somebody ought to warn her. I *hate* René, don't you?"

I made an ambiguous sound. I disliked René, but Freddy was a compulsive gossip, and anything you told him would be babbled all over the place by the end of the evening.

"Well, *I* do, and I'm not afraid to admit it," he said. "I mean, if I do, why not be frank about it? Don't you think so? I mean I simply *can not* stand him. So why shouldn't—"

"How's Mrs. Jones taking all this?" I asked.

Freddy rolled his eyes upward in an expression of combined awe and malice. "My dear!" he said. "*Fit* to be *tied*! What I'd *real*ly like, I'd like to see the two girls get together, both of them, and *turn* on René. Really, I don't know why some of these women don't simply dis*mem*ber him some time." He snickered parenthetically and said, "Can't you just *see* them *af*terward, *fight*ing over the choicer *parts*?" and then went on, "You know, I was sure Mrs. Jones was going to be *it*. Honestly, didn't you think he'd marry her? After all, anybody *could*! Practically everybody *has*! And she's still rich. Really, René *should*. You know he's getting on. Really quite pouchy under the eyes lately. Just notice some time. I mean he's really not going to have his looks for*ev*er, and there's always a new generation rising to com*pete* with, and—" but he stopped abruptly and said, "I refuse to talk about him. I simply refuse to *oc*cupy myself with him. Tell me about you, Hoopy. I do hope Italy was good, so you'll have *some*thing, because you *have* missed simply everything here. Was it good, Hoop? Italy?"

"Uh-huh."

"I'm so glad. Did you go to Capri?"

"Huh-uh."

"Well, why in the world *not*? *Ev*erybody goes to Capri now. Everybody always *has*! Then where in the world *did* you go?"

"Siena."

"But how medieval! Really, Hoop, you should have been a *school*teacher! A professor or something. You'd have been divine at it."

"Thanks."

"But I guess it's too late now, isn't it? What a shame."

"Yep."

"I can just see you in the schoolroom, all those eager little faces. *Too* medieval. I think our education's in a dreadful state, don't you? You simply don't belong in the modern world, Hoop, not going to Ca*pri*! And missing simply everything here. Tony's written a divine new song for Nicole."

"Simply?"

"What?"

"Don't you mean *sim*ply divine?"

"Well! Hoop! Really! That's unkind! I didn't expect it from *you*, I must say. Everybody thinks I'm such a fool, but I didn't think you did! I mean to say, you make me feel too too *et tu Brute* about it. *Do* you think I'm a fool, Hoopy?"

"Nope."

"Well, I'm so glad. Because I'm not, really. I know how I *sound*, and I know how I *act*. I know the im*press*ion I make. I know what everybody *thinks*! But it isn't true, I swear it isn't, and I thought you knew better. Just because I go around trying to keep on the bright side of things all the time. But what I mean is, why not? Why be dreary in public, is what I mean. Show a bright face to the world, at *least*, is the way I feel about it. Honestly, Hoop, when I'm alone I go through hell—absolute hell! I do, really. But I never get a bit of credit for it. Not a *bit*!"

So I told Freddy again, as I had told him many times before, that I didn't think he was a fool, because I didn't, even if he acted like one, and I told him I was certain that he went through hell, absolute hell, which I was, except that I was certain he went through it only in the upper brackets. He told me that he was so glad, that sometimes he thought I was the only person around who really under*stood* him.

"But you're right," he went on, "you're absolutely right, about Tony's song. It's not only divine, it *is* simply divine. Hoop, why don't you speak to Tony? I mean just put in a word or two for me? He's so much too good for this. He's got such a tremendous talent—genius, really. I've tried again and again, I've argued with him till I'm blue in the face—actually *blue*!—but it doesn't do a bit of good. He ought to quit all this and really study. You know, do serious things. I'd be happy to keep him. I really would! Here I am with all this *mon*ey and no *tal*ent—really—and there he is with all that *tal*ent and no *money*. You see how it dovetails. It *couldn*'t be neater! I mean it would make so much sense. And here he is, writing songs for a cheap singer—"

"Objection."

"Oh, all right, I know Nicole's good, she's *ter*ribly good, I ad*mire* her, and we all *love* her, especially *you*—and incidentally Hoopy there's quite a bit of *gos*sip, did you know? People saying you're absolutely *gone* on Nicole, really *sunk*, I mean in a while you're going to be nothing but an attachment of hers in people's thinking, I'd watch it if I were you, Hoopy, I really would, gossip can be so *vic*ious—but what I was saying, I'm as fond of Nicole as the next person, but she's simply devouring Tony, that's all there is to it, and it isn't fair. You can't abuse your talent in*def*initely without *cheap*ening it, is what I mean, and that's what's he's doing. Sometimes when I think about it I think I must, I simply must do something really *dras*tic about Tony, *any*thing to get him away from Nicole and really doing something important. Like Menotti or something. I can just see it, we could set up an apartment together and he could have his own workroom, a piano and everything. I mean the money wouldn't be anything to me, nothing at *all*. Quite the reverse. I always say, why shouldn't all this money made the way my father made it go to doing some real good for a change? I mean if a perfect upstart like my father makes all this *mon*ey, it's perfectly meaningless unless somebody else *does* something with it. Don't you think? We could have this apartment and I could sort of *nur*ture Tony. Do you see what I mean?"

"I'm afraid so."

"Now really, Hoop! I think you're being very unsympathetic. That's twice in ten minutes. I don't think Siena agreed with you at all. I mean if you're in a mood like this I guess you wouldn't think of saying anything to Tony for me, would you?"

"Nope."

"Well I'm not going to argue about it! I simply don't have the energy. But it's a rotten deal, it really is, Tony wasting himself around a place like this."

"You spend a lot of time around here yourself."

Freddy said, with one of those lapses into normal speech and comparatively straight thinking which kept occurring in the middle of his phrenetic chatter, "It's different with me, as of course you know. It doesn't make any difference what happens to me, any more than it makes any difference what happens to practically everybody else in the world. I'm nothing. Just nobody. I just happen to have all this money. Only one person in ten thousand is worth saving, and that's the person with talent. I mean real talent. I don't mean all these expatriate phonies."

He waited to see if I was really listening, and I looked at his silly attractive face and thought what a good face it might have been if the circumstances of Freddy's life had forced him towards strength and decision instead of all the bright vapid fluttering from which, I thought, it was too late for him to save himself. I said, "O.K., no objection."

Freddy said, "My mother goes around endowing all these orphans' homes and everything. But I always say, what difference do all those people make?"

"There's a theory that anybody with something to give the world will find a way to give it, without help."

"Hoop!" he cried out. "That's ridiculous! Don't say that! You *can't* say that! How do you know how much has been lost to the world because people like Tony have to do things like Tony's doing to stay alive? Look," he said, returning now to the refuge of his fluttering, "I'd *strang*le all those orphans, I mean with my own *hands*, if I thought it would help Tony. I really mean it! I'd *strang*le—"

"Now you're jabbering, Freddy."

"Honestly! You're im*poss*ible tonight. You really are! I simply won't—" but whatever he was going to say, he never said it, because the lights went down and the spot went on for Nicole and Tony.

"She's nearly twenty minutes late," I said to Freddy. "I've never known her to be late before."

"You just don't *know*," he murmured. "She's not herself at all. She's been quite distracted these last few days," he said, sounding pleased. "If it weren't for Tony..."

After I had finished telling her all this, Dr. Finney had very little to say about Bibi. "What's the best Bibi can hope for?" she asked, and I said that at the very best, Bibi might hope for a job as a charwoman.

"Like this old Bijou of Nicole's?"

"Not that good. Bijou's a housekeeper and almost a companion for Nicole at the club. Bibi couldn't ever take any responsibility."

"What makes you so sure Freddy's not a fool?"

I managed to make the jump from Bijou to Freddy, and said, "Because he's always having these lapses into good sense. A man with good sense can make a fool of himself now and then but a real fool can't lapse into good sense except maybe very occasionally by accident or imitation. And Freddy does it too frequently for it to be either."

Dr. Finney accepted this idea with a nod of her head, said she was getting hungry and wanted some more nourishment pretty soon, then asked, "What does he do in his spare time—besides nurture Tony? Does he have a whole stable of Tonys, or is Tony his only?"

"Tony's his only. And I've tried to tell you I'm not at all sure Freddy's what he appears to be. Spare time? He collects modern painting."

"Oh, my God! " said Dr. Finney. On the way into my room we had to go through the gallery, and it had taken only a glance at her face when she looked at my merchandise to know what she thought of it, outside of the fetishes.

"I know what you mean," I admitted, "but the hard fact is that Freddy's painting collection is the best reason I know to believe he's not a fool. Also, he's got a good heart under that fla-fla. Look. Half the paintings he buys are terrible, but he knows it. Half of them he buys because some poor devil is starving and Freddy's too sensitive to give a simple handout. But even so, he won't buy even these bad pictures from anybody unless he thinks there's some kind of talent there that's potentially worth saving. Like he said about all those orphans—he's not interested in anybody unless he's got talent. He'd watch them starve with complete indifference."

"If I want to keep Freddy on my list of suspects," Dr. Finney mused, "I have to balance his affection for Tony and his admiration for Tony's talent against his admiration for Nicole's talent. I suppose he'd admit, in the end, that she's pretty good?"

"Actually he thought as I thought, no matter what he said about her devouring Tony, that Nicole at her best has been damn near great. But anyway Freddy couldn't kill anybody. No matter what he said about strangling orphans. He could imagine it, but that's all."

"These Freddys can get pretty excited all of a sudden. They can be direct and vicious on the spur of the moment in a way they never could by premeditation. Suppose he came to see Nicole to try to talk her into releasing Tony, or something of the kind. Suppose she refused. Suppose she went on and told him what she thought of his probable private life. Suppose she relayed to him some comment or supposed comment from Tony as to what a nuisance Freddy was, always hanging around with intent to nurture. Can't you imagine Freddy beginning to scream and picking up a shovel and knocking Nicole out with it? I can."

"So can I. But I can't imagine Nicole doing all that."

Dr. Finney got up suddenly from the chair and began to pace uncomfortably up and down the room. "Dammit, I don't want to discuss all this," she said. "When all this stuff's only half formulated, it crystallises it to talk possibilities, and I'm not ready for it to crystallise yet. It closes things. Now what about the other half of Freddy's paintings?"

"They're good. He's got a real eye for a comer. He buys cheap at first exhibitions or even before the man's had a show, and he could probably double his investment already. And in the art racket, that's really something."

She kept pacing back and forth. I said, "What's wrong?"

"Freddy is," she said. "Also Audrey. Also Marie Louise. Also Tony. Also all these pictures. Also Nicole, not to mention René and Mrs. Jones. All these people. Bibi. Bijou. I feel out of my depth. No—it's worse. I've been out of my depth plenty of times, but now I feel out of my habitat. The Flea Club! Those other times, when I tried to figure things out this same way, I could feel it. And I could visualise it. Here, I can't. I don't know the places and I don't know this kind of life or these people. I'm such an outsider. All this Paris stuff. Boy," she said wryly, "am I ever a foreigner."

"People are pretty much the same everywhere," I suggested, not knowing whether I believe it or not.

"Nonsense," she said. "No, I take that back. They are. But they look so different against different backgrounds. Also, I'm starving."

I found a few crackers and some dried-up cheese and brought them out. I offered her wine to go with them, but she said no, more coffee. We settled down with this repast between us, and I kept talking.

CHAPTER SIX

WHEN TONY AND Nicole came out that night for their number, it was obvious that Freddy was right. Nicole was away off form. Tony sometimes accompanied her on the piano, sometimes on the accordion. Tonight it was the accordion, and the number, which I'd heard again and again, was virtually a duet between voice and instrument. It was a fine number, but Nicole wasn't doing much more than the most routine job. Even admitting that her routine job was a lot better than most people's good jobs, still there were a couple of tempo changes where she left Tony in the lurch, and he had to cover up for her. It wasn't obvious to everybody, but it was obvious to Freddy Fayerweather, and he punched me in the ribs with his elbow and said, "See? See what I mean? *Real*ly!"

They got a good hand, as usual, even so. Nicole took a couple of bows, made Tony take an extra bow himself, and they did two more numbers. Then the lights went up and Nicole came down from the small stage and began to walk around the place greeting people from table to table, as usual. What was less usual, Tony came along.

After a couple of preliminary pauses, they headed for the table where René sat with his Mrs. Jones.

From where Freddy and I stood, Mrs. Jones was nothing but a silhouette—narrow squared-off shoulders, a neck and a hat with a couple of faintly sinister feathers curling up from it into the smoky air. But I could imagine her poor raddled face that didn't look half bad if you caught her early enough in the evening, but began falling to pieces after the first couple of drinks. For Mrs. Jones and her ilk I am a chump. She was worthless, a parasite given to conspicuous waste, spoiled, even vicious, but I felt sorry for her. Poor Mrs. Jones with all those husbands and all that dough. I felt like going over and telling her not to worry—that if René was quitting her she was lucky, although of course it didn't make any real difference, since she had that infallible eye and unquenchable thirst for the real indisputable thoroughgoing dyed-in-the-wool good-looking son-of-a-bitch. She could pick them every time, and René might even be better than whatever was to follow.

Nicole and Tony paused and spoke to Mrs. Jones and then to René. After a minute or two Tony pulled up two chairs and they sat at the table. I noticed that René hadn't even stood up.

I turned to Freddy to say something or other which never got said, because he was looking as if he had been slapped across the face. He was pale and his lips were fluttering, and he was staring across at the group with an expression I'd have hated to have directed at me. "That *pros*titute! " he managed to whisper in a pathetic voice. "That *ab*solute *aban*doned *pros*titute! He's sitting down with that *ab*solute *pros*titute! "

"Oh, come now, Freddy. Poor Mrs. Jones."

"Mrs. Jones! Who's talking about Mrs. Jones? I mean *him*! René!" His voice had risen to a thin piercing treble.

"Freddy, for God's sake! "

"Well I don't care," he said, not much more quietly, and giving the impression of howling and wringing his hands. "I said it and I'll say it again for anybody to hear. I think René's an absolute prostitute! I think he's the most utterly des*pic*able—"

"*Des*picable."

"What?" He floundered for a minute. "Des*pic*able, *des*picable, what do I care? I *des*pise him and I say he's a *pros*titute!"

He looked ready to dissolve into tears, and when Freddy gets into a state like that you have to handle him carefully or there will be a real scene, so I began talking to him as calmly as I knew how. I told him that I agreed with him, that René was certainly a prostitute if the term included male courtesans near the top of their profession. "But look, Freddy," I said, "first of all, be generous. In lots of ways, René's exactly your opposite. It takes an effort of will to be fair."

"Well honestly, Hoop, if you're asking *me* to be fair to René—" and then, with sudden suspicion, "What do you mean, my opposite? Is that a crack?"

"Not at all. Look, Freddy, one thing you do share with René is an appetite for elegant living. But look at the difference. You came from nowhere, but you have an inexhaustible supply of money for clothes and automobiles and collecting paintings and so on. Isn't that true? You don't mind my saying it?"

"Of course not. I don't pretend to be anybody. I never *said* I was anybody, did I? I'm always saying I'm nobody, aren't I?"

"Good. That's a very sensible attitude, Freddy. But look at René. Gosh, Freddy, you ought to be sorry for him. He came from a really important somewhere. Family clear back to the Crusades. But your family from nowhere made a few million dollars out of the war, and René's lost the last penny they had. You say you haven't got a thing but money. René hasn't got a thing but six-feet-odd of beautiful body and the problem of feeding it."

"He's got something else, he's got entreé," Freddy said, and this was true. René had entreé to places Freddy and I couldn't have bought our way into with money *or* a body like René's and I suppose that except for a real talent of his own, the thing Freddy would have most liked to have was René's chichi connections.

"And anyway," Freddy objected further, "other people have to find a way to feed themselves, too, and they—"

"You don't."

"All right, I don't, but plenty of other people do, and they don't go and *pros*ti—"

"Listen, Freddy, it's a matter of using to best advantage whatever nature gave you. René's obvious answer is rich women until he finds that one rich wife, and René, being a Frenchman and practical, has adapted his life to his talents. That's all. He simply does what he does best, don't you see? It's logical."

I said it would be a crime to let exceptional equipment and training like René's go to waste. I said it was René's duty to use them. What a loss to the world, I suggested to Freddy, if Gieseking at René's age had decided to earn an honest living instead of playing the piano. How ridiculous, I pointed out, if Freddy's tailor should stop making suits for Freddy and take up the harp. So how absurd for René to get a job as a clerk instead of going to parties in Venetian palaces and getting bronzed on private beaches and skiing at Zermatt and other places too fancy for Freddy and me even to know about, and living on the Avenue George V instead of the Rue Bonaparte, pleasant as the Rue Bonaparte may be—not to mention the light and warmth he brought into the lives of one poor god-forsaken raddled weather-beaten broken-down money-ridden old she-dragon after another. It was not only René's privilege, I insisted to Freddy. It was his downright obligation.

Freddy looked at me, trying to decide whether I was meaning all this or not, and decided that there was a possibility that I did, and finally he said, "Really, Hoop, sometimes I think you're almost *too* broadminded." But I could see him accepting the proposition that if he expected people to tolerate his own conspicuous vagaries, he had to let them accept René's too, although it did seem to take some of the icing off the cake.

"Really, Hoop," he said again, "you quite depress me. *Nothing* is quite so depressing as logic when it works against you, is it? But of course I don't give a *damn*, I really don't, what René does, but I do hate to have Tony exposed to—"

"Tony's a child of the Paris streets. What he hasn't been exposed to, nobody has."

We were quiet for a minute. Freddy gazed into his highball glass and swirled the remains of his drink around in it absently, and then said to me, without looking up, "Hoop, once more. If you'd just *say* something to Tony for me, just suggest that if he devoted his talents entirely to serious work, you know, quit this place and let me set him up in a really good studio—"

"Absolutely not, once and for all. For one thing, Nicole would never forgive me."

"You're just crazy about that old Nicole," he said. "Everybody is, and nobody really appreciates Tony. I don't want to talk to you any more tonight, you're too depressing. Not going to Ca*pri*, and all this rot about René's *du*ty to *pros*titute himself. You don't fool me one bit."

He set his glass down and turned as if to leave without looking at me, but then he turned back, looked at me directly and smiled, and said, "No hard feelings."

"Of course not, Freddy." Impossible to hold any hard feelings against Freddy.

"And if Tony comes over here, at least suggest that I want to see him at my table, will you?"

"O.K., Freddy, I'll do that."

"Really, Hoop," Freddy said, "you're very nice. Sometimes I think you're the *on*ly one around here who understands me."

By the time I had told all this to Mary Finney, it was getting well along into the early morning, two or three o'clock. I croaked, "I'm tired! I've got to have a breather."

"How about a brief refreshing walk through beautiful Paris? A few lungfuls of nice cold Luxembourg air?"

"Closed at night."

"Tuileries, then. Relax you. Walk and talk."

"But I can't talk! My throat—"

"You talk to me the rest of tonight, see, then maybe we can catch a couple of hours sleep, then I want to talk to some of these people, first thing tomorrow. Think I could?"

"Some of them would see us if I asked them. Your little French friends could manage the others by less friendly persuasion, if you're serious. Haven't you got the keys to the city or something?"

"Just so I get to see them. Come on," she said, "pull yourself together. We'll walk a little. Freshen us up. What else happened that night?"

"I had a brush with Nicole. I learned something about Audrey that shocked me, and I met the Italian boy."

As for the brush with Nicole…

She and Tony came over to the bar to say hello, and I gave Tony Freddy's message. He went to Freddy's table. Freddy leaned across the table and talked earnestly, as if there had been no interruption in their conversation, and Tony sat there as usual, looking enigmatic and gentle.

Nicole and I said a few odds and ends about Siena and so forth. Then I said, "What's happened around here? Anything new?"

"No, nothing. How did I sing tonight?"

"You're always good."

"But not as good tonight as some times?"

"Maybe not inspired."

"I'm tired," she admitted. "I haven't been sleeping."

"Troubles?"

She hesitated long enough for it to be a confession, then said, "No, not really."

I took a shot in the dark, for no reason that I can remember except that Freddy had been talking about him: "How's my friend René?"

"I didn't know you called René your friend."

"'Friend' is just a manner of speaking. I hear he has a new woman."

Nicole said with great control, "Freddy talks too much."

"Poor guy, he's jealous. Freddy suffers, you know."

"Any person with money who suffers is a fool."

"Gosh, Nicole, that's a broad statement."

She shrugged. I went on, "Freddy seems to think René shouldn't bring his women around here," which was ridiculous, of course. "Seems to think he ought to ply his trade elsewhere."

Nicole never drank. She had just then, as usual, a glass of rather awful lemon soda. She set it down so suddenly that some of it slopped over on to her hand. I pulled out a handkerchief, but she rejected it. She was silent, cold and removed from me, while the bartender brought a towel. She wiped her hand carefully, pushed away the towel, looked at me and said very deliberately, "Freddy talks too much. So, for the first time, do you," and she left, walking away, through the room, and past the stage to the door which led back of it.

Over at his table, René rose. He walked round the table and pulled Mrs. Jones's chair out for her as she rose also. She was hidden by René's back; then, as they started moving away from the table, I saw her face.

It wasn't Mrs. Jones at all. It was Audrey.

René had a new one, and it was Audrey.

On the other hand, Audrey had a new one, and it was René.

Suddenly I felt better. It was like the opening of a fight before the gong has rung, where you have no favourite but are sure either fighter deserves the worst that can happen to him, and that whatever happens is going to be brutal and bloody. Not that I've ever seen such a fight, but I had that kind of feeling.

I turned round quickly and hunched myself over the bar. If they were leaving, they would have to pass right by me. I didn't ask myself why I didn't want Audrey to see me, but I didn't. I didn't want to have to talk to her. Then I realised that maybe I did have a favourite in this fight after all. I was sorry for anybody that got mixed up with René, even sorrier than I was for anybody who got mixed up with Audrey.

Audrey and René didn't leave the Club, though. Instead, they went over to the door that led into the members' cellar and I saw René get out his key, unlock it, and stand aside for Audrey, who went on through the door and started down the stairs. René looked up and caught my eye and nodded. That was all right, Audrey hadn't seen me.

I suppose it was fifteen or twenty minutes later that Tony got up and left Freddy's table, just a minute or two before Mrs. Jones appeared.

I am not sure that anybody would ever have called Mrs. Jones a real beauty, and I never saw her except in newspapers and magazines until she was already pushing into middle age, but I have seen her when she was still a good-looking woman, from a slight distance. I have also seen her when she looked like a beat old hag even from a long way off. She was a beat old hag when she came into The Flea Club that night looking for René. Her clothes and hair gave a general effect of disarray, and her face had had a serious quarrel with her make-up.

She came in alone by the boulevard entrance, ducking in quickly as if escaping from somebody, glanced quickly around the room, and finally fixed me with a gaze at once intense and vague. Mrs. Jones had met me half a dozen times around The

Flea Club, and a couple of times I had been at the same table with her, but she never remembered my name and she never more than half remembered my face. I am rather a plain honest type, not at all the type she responded to. But this time she established some kind of association between me and René. After the fifth or sixth drink, Mrs. Jones's mental switchboard tended to break down. It was never possible to tell just what final connection would result from an original impulse.

She came up to me exuding a typical aroma of gin and cosmetics and said, "All right, where is he?"

"Who?"

"You know who," she said, and it was the truth. "René."

"Mrs. Jones, I've no idea."

"Why don't you call me Hattie? You always have," she said. I had never used her first name in my life. "Where's René?"

"I said I didn't know."

"I know you did. But I know you do."

"Well, I don't. Will you have a drink with me instead—Hattie?"

"I'm on the wagon," she said so firmly that I think she believed it. "Anyway I've asked you time and time again not to call me Hattie and I wish you wouldn't."

"Just as you say. What do you want René for?"

"I want to tear him to pieces. I've got a piece of news for that son-of-a-bitch."

"You have really?"

"Oh, nothing he doesn't already know. But something he doesn't know I know."

"I don't suppose you'd tell me? I'd be happy to deliver the message."

"Certainly not. I have few enough pleasures in life as it is. Did he have that woman with him?"

"Concerning René that's a vague question. Which woman?"

"Audrey, her name is. She's nobody, of course—nobody at all. Trying to crash, of all the nerve. I know what people are saying, of course. They're saying René jilted me for her. Isn't that true? I mean what they're saying. Because it isn't true." She looked at me huffily as if I had argued with her and said, "It may interest you to know I jilted René."

"Oh, it does. It fascinates me. I never doubted it."

"You're sweet, sometimes. Now where are they?"

"I really don't—"

"You're horrible," she said, and there was nothing casual left in her voice when she added, "You can go straight to hell," and she started for the cellar entrance.

Freddy came tootling up to me from across the room, piping "Oh, my *dear*! Witches' Sabbath, no less! *Just* what I've always wanted to happen. Been *wait*ing for! Hoopy, come *on*, let's not *miss* it!" He grabbed my arm and we crossed the room. By the time we got to the cellar door Mrs. Jones had her purse open and was fumbling around in it for her keys, but before she could find them, Freddy produced his own and opened up for her.

"You're so right, Hattie," he said. "You're so absolutely *right*. What I mean is, why let René play fast and loose with you? It's your *dig*nity, is what I mean, don't you think? Because after all, think who *you* are—but who is *he*? And as for this Audrey thing, I think you're so right, *so* right, and I'd tear her to pieces if I were you, I'd have no com*punc*tion in your position, none at *all*..." and as they went down the stairs his voice trailed away. Fragments of sentences floated behind him like so many chiffon veils: "... ordinary *clim*ber, that's...be so *bitch*y about it...absolutely *justi*fied, no com*punc*tion, and no *mer*cy, my dear..."

By this time I had stopped thinking the situation was funny and was beginning to get scared. I didn't care if Mrs. Jones and Audrey got into an old-fashioned hairpull with Freddy as referee, but I did care about Nicole and her club. This was exactly the kind of thing she was afraid of, even if it happened in the relative privacy of the members' cellar. I didn't feel like stepping in between the two principals so I decided to go right to Nicole herself and tell her things were about to pop.

I hurried to the little room back of the stage which served as its wings, and was also the entrance hail to Nicole's upstairs apartments, with her stairs going up out of it. Tony, with his coat and shoes off, was lying on the small couch which with a chair and mirror and diminutive dressing-table made up the furnishings of the place. I told him what was going on, as quickly as I could. Nicole was upstairs, he said, and when I hesitated—because I had never been up there—he said he would go up and tell Nicole I wanted to see her.

He had hardly left when Mrs. Jones burst in on me, looking really awry now, with Freddy close behind her, flushed with excitement. "...couldn't have gone *far*," he was babbling, "...saw them go down there not fifteen minutes ago, I *know*."

Mrs. Jones looked at me without any recognition at all. Then her eye lit on the stairway. "What's that?" she demanded. "Where does that go?"

"Upstairs! " Freddy shrieked, losing all control. "Right upstairs to the *bedroom*! Honestly it gets better and better! Worse and worse, Hattie dear. Honestly, if *Nicole's* in on this *too*, I think it's just too *good*, I mean I didn't think she'd go *that* far, but if they're not in the *cellar*, where *else*—"

Mrs. Jones's feet must have touched the stairs but that isn't the way I remember it. I remember her as just being lifted off the floor and sucked up the stairway in one swift movement, like a piece of paper up a chimney. There was a banging, a fist pounding on a door up there. Freddy uttered a cry of sheer incredulous ecstasy, and disappeared up the stairs in much the same manner as Mrs. Jones. There was a moment's silence, then the sound of voices in which I could recognise Nicole's and Mrs. Jones's, growing louder and, in Mrs. Jones's case, recriminative. She began then to scream, a shrill, thin, furious sound, half hysterical. A door was banged shut, muffling the screams, but they still trickled through, a horrifying sound. Apparently the room they had gone into was directly over my head. The thin screaming sound now began to be confused with the sound of scraping and thumping on the floor, a struggle of some kind, and that was when I went up the stairs myself.

There were two doors on the landing, both closed. I opened the first one at hand, which proved to be to Nicole's living-room. Freddy was bouncing around its periphery, bug-eyed with delight at the spectacle in the centre of the room. Tony stood there, his face red with the strain, his arms locked around Mrs. Jones from behind, while she writhed and screamed. Nicole stood in front of her, slapping her first on one cheek and then on the other, deliberately but hard, saying, "Now stop!" then a slap, "Now stop that!" then a slap, then "Stop that!"

I closed the door and went back to the bar. It was an awful thing to have seen, and I kept seeing it. I could see Mrs. Jones still; she seemed to get more and more slippery as she writhed in Tony's embrace, and that was the awful thing—it began to be an embrace, and the whole thing began to turn erotic on me. I didn't like it much. I didn't like it at all.

It wasn't more than ten minutes, though, before Nicole came into the bar, obviously looking for me, and motioned to me to come. We went into the little backstage room.

"Anything I can do, Nicole?"

"You can say nothing about all this."

"Of course. What's going on up there now?" There was no more sound.

"She is lying down. Tony is with her until I get back. I think she has—what you call it, passed out. Whatever made her think she might have found René in my rooms?"

"Just crazy, I guess. Apparently René and this other woman left by the back door?"

"I suppose so. Thank you, Hoop, but there's nothing you can do, no. We will call her car to get her home. This kind of thing is very terrible, of course. I will not sing well in this next performance."

"Yes you will. You're always good. But I don't think I'll hang around tonight, if there's really nothing I can do to help."

"There isn't. Good night, Hoop."

As for the Italian boy...

I met him at the boulevard door, as I left the club.

He was around twenty years old, of medium height, very dark as to hair and eyes, but not swarthy. His face showed that combination of arrogance, sensuality, alertness, and quick good will which makes it so difficult for me to decide whether I like Italians or Frenchmen best. His suit was new and respectable, but neither expensive nor fashionable. He was standing at the side of the door, and as I started along the boulevard he took a few quick steps to catch me, and said, "Sir—excuse me, but is it very expensive in there?"

"Depends what you mean, expensive. Five hundred francs for a drink at the bar." That was close to a dollar and a half at the legal rate, and if your native coin was the lira, it was steep.

"Can anyone go in?"

"I could get you in. Shall I? Nicole's worth the price?"

"What is?"

"Nicole, the singer. Haven't you heard of her?"

He hadn't, which made it odd that he should be hanging around outside The Flea Club, with half a dozen more promising-looking places in the neighbourhood.

"I'd like to go in for a while," he decided. I scribbled a note on a card, with the date, wrote "Bearer introduced for this night," signed it, and gave it to him. Then I went along the boulevard to the Rue Bonaparte and turned down it towards my place.

I was followed.

Dr. Finney hung over the rail of the Pont des Beaux Arts. Her breath rose in moonstruck vapour as she contemplated the river purling beneath her. At this ungodly hour of the morning the water was nearly flat, undisturbed by any river traffic; only the supports of the bridge, butting gently against the currents, raised a few long, spreading ripples. According to which tradition you chose to follow, she might have been contemplating suicide, pondering the mysteries of life, or composing a poem. As it turned out, she was occupied with thoughts of a sweet, gaseous, citron-flavoured beverage.

"Tell me about Nicole's lemon sodas," she said.

"She never drank anything stronger. Wine at meals, of course, but no cocktails, no highballs—nothing, ever."

"Is that so unusual, in a Frenchwoman?"

"Not except for the rigour she enforced it on herself with. It wasn't a matter of taste so much as inviolable rule."

"I see. She ever say as much to you?"

"Come to think of it, no. I guess it was just obvious or something."

"I see," Dr. Finney repeated, and then, "I'm inclined to accept that."

She stood silently for a while, watching the river, while I got colder. Then, "Did you notice, Hoop, when we went into the cellar this morning, there was a bottle of lemon soda open on one of the tables, with a glass—an inch or so of the stuff in the glass, too, and some whisky and soda with ice in another glass, and a bottle of whisky and a seltzer bottle?"

"No, I didn't. You sent me upstairs so quick to look—"

"Well, there was. All these people you know around The Flea Club, the ones you've told me about so far—would any of them be ruled out because they wouldn't have been drinking whisky that early in the morning?"

"It'd be damn funny if any of them were there so early in the morning, whisky or no whisky. Bunch of night owls. Maybe the glasses were left over from the night before."

"The place hadn't been straightened up yet, that's true," Dr. Finney admitted, "but the ice wasn't melted in the glass, and the soda hadn't lost its fizz."

"I've lost mine," I said. "Let's call it a night. Let me take you to your hotel. I'm tired out and freezing to death."

"We'll go back to your place and turn up the heater. I'd suggest that palace I'm staying in but we might keep Emmy awake. Also, no coffee-maker. Come on," she said, and we started back again.

Dr. Finney continued, "I don't know much about night-club singers but it seems to me that Nicole leads an extraordinarily quiet and circumspect life for any young and vigorous woman who's successful and on her own. What about lovers?"

"None."

"So far as you know."

"So far as anybody knows."

"Seems odd."

"It *is* odd."

"Maybe there's a very secret one."

"I don't think so."

"René, for instance."

"I can't believe it."

"Emotionally?"

"No," I said; "reasonably. René's not a sensualist, particularly. And if he did want it for excitement he can get them younger and prettier than Nicole. The point is, he's in the business, and he can also get them older and richer, which is his special forte. And it's impossible from Nicole's point of view. She knows exactly what René is, wouldn't get mixed up with him emotionally, and she's a hard-headed business woman herself. She's not going to pay for it."

"You've got it all figured out, haven't you?"

"I've thought about it before."

"All very odd," she said. "There wouldn't be any stigma attached to her having a lover, would there? Wouldn't it be quite usual?"

"Quite."

"But she absolutely hasn't?"

"You keep insisting. All I can say is that even Freddy Fayerweather admits she hasn't. If there were ever a whisper, Freddy would hear it. And if there were ever a lover, there'd be a whisper."

"What about Tony?"

"With Nicole? Never."

"Why not? Lots of sympathy there. Both coming up the hard way, both talented, lots of propinquity. Don't tell me Tony's an ascetic."

"Tony's got a private life none of us know anything about."

"How do you know that?"

"Well—I guess I don't know it. He just disappears into some world of his own when The Flea Club closes, and he's such a quiet fellow I've always taken it for granted that he had things satisfactorily organised. Anyway, about him and Nicole, if they were lovers I suppose they might be able to conceal it in conversation and so on, but never when they were doing a song together."

"Why, Hoopy!" said Dr. Finney, "you're a romantic!"

We went on back to my place then, and by the time we were settled, with the heater going full blast, and the coffee made, and Dr. Finney with her stockinged feet propped up before her, and me in an old bathrobe that had been my dearest friend ever since adolescence, I knew that what I wanted to do more than anything else was to go on talking to her all night, because I began to feel (rather than see) that everything I was saying was really going to tie in, before long, with what had happened that morning in the cellar of The Flea Club. So I took my own shoes off and propped my feet up like Mary Finney's, and started talking again.

CHAPTER SEVEN

I HAD MET Audrey Bellen Saturday morning, met the plane bearing Mary Finney and Emily Collins Saturday afternoon, taken Marie Louise to the Opera Saturday night, and thereafter had gone to The Flea Club as I related. Sunday morning I slept until a reasonable hour and fooled around for a little while straightening up the gallery and getting it ready to open again on Monday, since it had been closed while I had been away. Then I went to St. Sulpice for the services, since Marcel Dupré was the organist, and I looked at the two Delacroix murals near the entrance and wondered why I never managed to get any excitement out of them when so many other people claimed they did. I decided they were bluffing. From St. Sulpice it was natural to gravitate back along the street to the Deux Magots for a little quiet spectating, but once there, to my own surprise, I telephoned Marie Louise.

I recognised the voice of the pomaded young man when I asked for Mrs. Bellen's suite. Who was calling, please? Mr.

Taliaferro, for Miss Bellen. One moment, please. Then Marie Louise's voice.

"Hello." It was the same indifferent hello she had given me when she walked into the lobby the night before.

"Good morning," I said. "It's Hooper Taliaferro. How you feeling?"

There was a short pause, heavily laden with nothing, and then she said, "Soggy."

"Too bad. I hope it clears up. Ever been to Lipp's?"

"No, I haven't. The places you go to have such funny names. First The Flea Club, now Lipp's."

It was a long speech compared to what she had given me so far. I said, "It's a nice place for lunch. I offer it to you."

"You don't have to do that," she said.

In the background I very clearly heard Audrey say, "Who is it, dear?"

I said, "I do have to eat, though. How about it?"

"Oh, no. I don't think so. Thanks, but I don't think so."

More Audrey in the background, but unintelligible. Then Marie Louise, "Oh, *Ma*ma!" in exasperation, and then some murmur back and forth. Then Audrey: "Hello, Hoop? Well how really sweet of you to call! Marie Louise had a perfectly lovely time last night, and I—now what was it you wanted?"

"I wanted Marie Louise for lunch, but it seems sort of complicated."

"But of course she'll come to lunch. She'd be delighted."

I heard Marie Louise quite clearly: "I won't I won't I won't and I won't!" Things began to get out of control on the other end of the wire and I just stood listening to the hubbub. There was a silence, then some real noise—a sort of running, and voices raised and talking both at once.

Then Audrey all at once, frantic: "Hello, hello—"

"Hello, Audrey."

"Hello, this is Mrs. Bellen. My daughter just started downstairs. Will you stop her, please—Audrey? Who said

Audrey? Oh, Hoop—Hoop, please hang up, hang up right now. Call me back, will you? *Hang up*!"

Five minutes later, nobody answered the telephone in Mrs. Bellen's suite. Ten minutes later, the pomaded young man told me that Mrs. Bellen and Miss Bellen were both out. I asked that Mrs. Bellen call Mr. Taliaferro at the Deux Magots if she got in within the next hour, and ten minutes later, she did.

"Hoop, I'm so sorry. Things became dreadfully confused. Now where were we?"

"I wanted Marie Louise for lunch, then hell broke loose. Sorry. I didn't know it was going to crack everything up."

"But it didn't. What do you mean?"

"I thought things sounded pretty complicated there for a while."

"Marie Louise decided to go out, that's all, and—there was something I wanted to tell her before she got away, though, and so—that's all it was. I'm sorry if we sounded terribly noisy and American and common about everything," she said, with a pretty laugh that showed how very, very uncommon she was. "Poor little Hoopsy, all puzzled at the other end of the line!"

"Yeah. Well, I guess that's all." The last person I wanted to see was Audrey, but in decency I had to say, "I don't suppose you're free for lunch yourself?"

"Well, how sweet! How really sweet! I do think it's the sweetest idea in the world. But I can't do it. Listen, Hoop—" pause, and a shift from pure sugar to something conspiratorial in suggestion—"call Marie Louise again, won't you? I know she'd love to go somewhere with you again. She's awkward about these things. I'm sorry about just now—really—but call her again. Call her tomorrow."

"Thanks, I will."

"Do that, without fail. Good-bye, Hoop."

"So long."

I hung up, visualising Audrey at the Prince du Royaume hanging up and then beginning to walk the floor, back and forth, up and down, around and about. The tension had never gone out of her voice.

But I didn't get a chance to call back, because Audrey called me first. I ate alone at Lipp's, then went back to the gallery and did some more straightening up, then lay down to read. My phone rang and there she was.

"Hoop, I've got to see you. I know it's going to sound perfectly crazy but I must. Now don't tell me you're busy this afternoon."

"I'm free, more or less."

She became a little arch, really working to get me. "I won't listen to any of your maybes! I've a perfectly delightful surprise for you and we'll make it a party, a real party. A cocktail party, in your honour. Will you come to my very special cocktail party in your honour this afternoon, Hoop?"

"Sure. When?"

"Early, so we'll have plenty of time together. Five."

"Five's all right."

Laughter and charm, then, "I'm so happy about it! It's a wonderful surprise, and ever and ever so special. Five."

"O.K. Five."

"Five! Until five—Hoop."

Somebody had to stop it. I said good-bye and hung up.

It seemed to me that Audrey was getting a little out of hand. Yesterday morning she had finagled me into that date. Last night I had caught her at The Flea Club with a prize bastard. This morning I had listened in on a big row of some kind between her and her daughter, and now she wanted me for something and she was so eager to have me that she was sounding plenty silly and artificial about it, apparently on the assumption that in order to get me she had to do it the hard way. What to expect at five for my delightful surprise, I had no idea.

At five I was walking down the corridor towards her suite. The hardest test of a hotel is its corridors. This one was immaculate, and there was something special about the air in it. The carpet caressed the soles of your feet right through your shoes. The door to Audrey's suite was bone white and martini gold, and the mounting for the push button suggested minuets at the Petit Trianon. I gave it a rude punch anyway; there was a chaste response somewhere back in the apartment. The door opened and there she was. Audrey. In person.

No maid, no guests, no Marie Louise. Just Audrey, in a crisp black dress of some kind with threads of green and violet here and there, in a little hallway with white and gold walls and a grey carpet and a big bunch of pink roses on a little table, doubled in the mirror behind them. Beyond the hallway there was a glimpse of a living-room, shadowy in the early-evening light, with lamps lit, suggestive of luxurious intimacy. There was even a real fire in an undersized, delicately carved marble fireplace. The silence was impregnated with the impression of twenty-dollar gold pieces flowing unnoticed down the drain.

"Hoopy!" Audrey murmured. I had met her a little more than twenty-four hours before, and so far as she knew I had seen her only once, but her tone suggested a lifetime of intimacy between us, with many many happy intimate years to follow—especially this afternoon. She murmured, "Perfectly delightful," and I was as suspicious as hell.

The way she closed the door behind us was like whispering a secret. I followed her into the living-room. There were bottles and glasses on a little table by a couple of chairs. More roses, breathing their scent into the room like so much life blood, and a faint suggestion of another scent—Audrey herself, bathed and sweetened for the sacrifice.

Little bits of golden light trembled in the vermouth. If this is a make, I thought, it's going to have to be awfully quiet and elegant. It would be a shame if anybody got rowdy. A sigh, perhaps a little shudder—nothing more.

"I thought it was a party," I said.

She looked at me and murmured, "It is. Just you and me. I told you it was ever so special."

It was all so exquisite and precious that something was going to have to crack soon. She made a little motion towards the fireplace, crossing and sinking into one of a pair of chairs there, while her dress rustled confidence as to how delightful Audrey was within it. I sat in the other chair and she raised her eyebrows faintly as she gestured towards the table, meaning would I mix a little something, and I began combining ice and gin and vermouth. She smiled and nodded *yes* when I looked at her, and half whispered to me the single word, *lemon*. It was another secret. Just between me and her. She liked lemon in her martinis, and she had let me in on it.

I began wondering what would happen if I said something really vulgar, such as, "Audrey, this is a lot of crap. What do you want?" I began wondering so hard that after a couple of minutes, I said it. I had never used the word to a woman before.

She laughed brightly, but this time it came out in pieces. She said, "Well! Really! Mr. Taliaferro! How very direct!"

"I'm a direct type boy. It isn't that I don't appreciate all this. I do. But it's such a long way around."

She looked at me hard for a minute, hunting a cue, and then she reached with great deliberation towards an enamelled box on the table and took a cigarette from it. I started for a match but she shook her head and waved me off, and lit it for herself, not making a minuet of it now, but lighting it to get it lit, the way a man would. She took one long thoughtful drag and held the smoke in her lungs until my own began to feel strained, then she blew it out into the room, killing the scent of the roses and knocking hell out of the mood she had been building up. Then she stubbed the cigarette out and dropped it in the ashtray and leaned back, looking at me with a half-smile but not a phony one, and said in a cool voice, "I haven't quite figured you out, after all. That was a little offensive."

"I guess it was," I said. "I apologise a little."

"Don't bother."

I poured two drinks and picked up one and offered it to her. She took the glass, said, "Thanks, Hoop," and set it down in front of her. She didn't touch it again. I took a sip or two of mine, and then she said, "Very well. It's about Marie Louise. She's taken quite a shine to you."

"Come again?"

She repeated exactly: "It's about Marie Louise. She's taken quite a shine to you."

"Marie Louise has? To me?"

"Yes," she said, almost irritably, then controlled herself and said, "You're surprised?"

"More than surprised. I find it hard to believe."

"So do I. Not that you're unattractive, I don't mean that. But it isn't like Marie Louise."

"How not?"

"It's a long story and a little complicated."

"Go ahead and tell it, if you want to."

"Of course I want to. That's what I got you up here for."

I asked, "Where's Marie Louise now?"

"Out. I left her at a movie. She's alone. And that shows how important this is. I'm not supposed to let her be alone at all, but I didn't know how else to talk to you. I'm picking her up for dinner, and I'm staying in tonight to be with her. Will you have dinner with us?"

"I don't know. Are you asking me again to baby-sit afterwards?"

"Don't be rude, Hoop. There's nothing in it for either of us that way. I wanted to go about all this more gracefully, but you chose another tone. I've been so worried all day. I'm trying to tell you these things, and it isn't easy. It's just that all of a sudden you've come to occupy a—rather special place in our lives, or anyway, you could, and—oh, I don't know! Everything's so unexpected and difficult."

She seemed to be having real difficulty, and it allayed my suspicions. I was certain she was a facile liar, and if she was really having all this trouble saying what she wanted to, maybe she was trying to tell the truth. She knit her brows, adding five years to her age, reached for a cigarette, and then crumpled it and threw it in the fire without lighting it.

"Listen," she said at last, as if she had reached an agreement with herself, "I'll be as direct as I can about it. I suppose it won't sound any less strange if I try to approach it head on. And I won't blame you if you just say no to the whole thing. I really won't. Believe that. Although I hope you'll say yes."

Long pause, then more slowly, "I've had a lot of trouble with Marie Louise lately. Maybe you've heard whispers of it. That's why we're here—in Europe, that is. She's depressed to the point of needing psychiatric attention. There's not a reason in the world for it—she's pretty, as you can see. We're wealthy and she can have everything she wants. She's always been attractive to boys, so much so that I've had a very difficult time managing things, and until lately she's had a good healthy interest in them. When this new thing began to develop, I got so worried about her that I had psychiatrists to the house, passing them off as guests, and they all said the same thing. She's not over the edge, but she's near it. Anything could—could push her over the edge, any time. I don't want analysis for her because I'm convinced that at this stage it could do more harm than good. I don't think she has any suspicion things are as dangerous as they are. And if you breathe a single word of this to her, I swear I'll kill you."

She hadn't looked directly at me all this time and she didn't look directly at me now. She seemed to be thinking over what she had said, and then she did look at me, and said, "You understand that? I'll kill you. Shall I go on?"

"Yes. Please do."

"All right. I thought maybe if we made this trip I could pull her out of it. So far as I can see it hasn't done a bit of good. Sometimes she's worse, if anything. I've done everything I know how—we've bought enough clothes to last for years, we've seen every show in town, we've flown to London and Rome and everything else, but none of it does any good. Maybe I'm not any good at the job. But it seems to me I've offered the best there is to be had in the way of diversion—and it doesn't take. What do you think?"

"You're asking me right in the middle."

"I know. What do you think, anyway?"

"Mostly I think I'd be bored stiff in Marie Louise's place."

"Bored stiff!" she cried. "Really, Hooper, if she's bored with all this I'm sure I don't know—"

"I mean that if she's bored with a week of it, three months of it is just that much worse. You haven't said so, but I imagine in Rome you bought clothes and went to everything you could get tickets for and so on, and the same in London, and so on. It's all been just more of the same thing, hasn't it?"

"Oh, I see that! " she said. "Of course I understand that! But it's so abnormal! And the thing is, she's met dozens of people, some of the most attractive young men you can imagine, and she's simply impossible about it. She refuses to go out with them, or if she does she comes home and says she's had a perfectly miserable time. The way she did with you."

"Yes, ma'am," I said with feeling. "The way she did with me."

"She said it was perfectly dreadful."

"You told me this morning she had such a lovely time."

Audrey brushed this aside with a gesture, and went on, "Perfectly dreadful. And that's what's so odd. That's where you come in. This morning she told me how perfectly dreadful last night had been, one of the very worst, she said, and when I suggested that I call you and ask you for dinner, as a return for your kindness, she said no, absolutely not, that she didn't want to see you again, ever. We had an awful scene about it. Then you telephoned, right in the middle of it, and I suppose you know what happened."

"Not exactly."

"I simply asked her who it was on the phone, as politely as possible, I must say, and when she said she would absolutely not see you, naturally I took the telephone and tried to patch things up. Isn't that perfectly natural?"

I passed that one up, and she went on, "Then when I was talking to you she was pacing around the room and all of a sudden she absolutely bolted. She absolutely tore out into the hall and grabbed her coat and simply bolted out of the place. Well of course that was dreadful, because in her condition I always insist that she mustn't go out alone."

"Perfectly natural," I interpolated.

She took it straight and said, "Of course. Then I was positively frantic, because how did I know what she was going to do, jump in the Seine or something, and there I was, not even dressed, I had on a housecoat and couldn't possibly have followed her, even if I could have caught up with her. I did run out into the hall, but she was already tearing down the stairs—didn't even wait for the elevator, mind you. Then I came running back—it was all so frantic—to try to get them to stop her at the desk, and there you were; still hanging on the line. By the time I got rid of you, of course she had got clear out of the hotel, and by the time I had put on a dress and got out on to the sidewalk, she wasn't in sight anywhere. And that was that."

"All very exciting," I said, "but it still doesn't sound as if she had taken quite a shine to me."

"I'm coming to that. Well, you can imagine how I felt. I just didn't know what to do. When you called back and I had to carry on that silly conversation as if everything was all right, I thought I would absolutely scream. I kept thinking of her throwing herself in the Seine and everything, although of course she's an excellent swimmer, and—"

"That mink coat of hers would sink anybody."

"She didn't wear the mink, she wore her black cloth," Audrey said, straight. She was a tough audience for gags that afternoon. "—and I was on the verge of calling the police, when in she walked. After leaving me with no word at all and nearly insane, nearly two hours. And what she'd been doing, I suppose I'll never know."

"Didn't she say."

"Oh, yes, she *said*, all right, but naturally I didn't believe her," Audrey said impatiently. "She came stalking in the door looking like death itself, and she wouldn't say a thing to me except that she wanted to be left alone, and when I asked her what she had been doing she said she had gone to a café and had a cup of chocolate and sat there trying to think things out! I don't believe that for a minute. She said she had other things to decide, and for me please to leave her alone. Well, I did, although I didn't quit the apartment, you can be sure of that. I even had our lunches brought up and—I know it was silly, but I kept feeling afraid she might try to jump out of the window or something—cut her wrists or something, I've heard of things like that. But she seemed quite calm, when I would go into her room to see how she was. She was simply lying on the bed, and said she was trying to think things out, and really she seems to have done it. She suddenly appeared all dressed and freshened up and apparently in quite good spirits, and she told me that she had decided you were a most attractive man and that she wanted to see you again."

"Me?"

"Yes."

"You're sure? Hoop Taliaferro?"

"Yes. Isn't it fantastic?"

"She didn't go into any detail?"

"Not exactly. Only in the most general way, that is. Only that you were nice-looking—which you are, Hoop, quite nice-looking, although I wish you'd stand better, and you ought to get that suit pressed—and extremely sympathetic, she said—which goodness knows I must say you haven't been to me, especially, but that is beside the point—and that she hoped very much you would take her out again. Now isn't that extraordinary?"

"I don't get it at all."

"Neither do I. I'm just telling you what happened. So I told her I'd ask you to dinner some time soon, which would be the perfectly natural and normal thing to do socially, and we would hope for the best after that, but then she began to get terribly disturbed again, and said no, she wanted to go out with *you*, she didn't want to have you to dinner with me there. Well, I was awfully put out with her. After all, I was doing my best and getting very little thanks for it, but I was handling her with kid gloves, absolute kid, and told her for goodness' sake what did she expect, did she expect you to call again, after the way she had treated you on the phone that morning?"

Audrey made a helpless gesture. "So that's the way we left it, that there was nothing to do but for me to ask you to dinner so you would maybe reciprocate and ask her out later, but she said she thought she would die in the meantime, and I almost think I would too, Hoop, I'm so curious to find what it's all about. So then I was really terribly clever. I sat down and wrote you a note inviting you to dinner, and told her I was going out to mail it. But I wasn't, I was going out to telephone you to come here this afternoon, since I couldn't do it with Marie Louise in the room. And I did."

"And here I am."

"Yes. So I took her and left her at this movie—where I ought to be picking her up right now, by the way. Naturally I didn't tell her I was going to urge you to take her out. But I do, Hoop, I beg you. Of course you can take me up on that dinner invitation too. I mailed it, but I beg you to take Marie Louise out."

"What's my wonderful wonderful surprise?"

"What surprise?"

"The one I was going to get at this cocktail party."

"Why, that Marie Louise likes you so much, silly!"

"Oh, Audrey. Baloney."

"All right, take it any way you please. I talked that way because I wanted to be sure you'd come, that's all. Now I've told you all of it."

I sat there trying to make head or tail out of this rigmarole, without much luck, even by making liberal allowance for Audrey's lying, which was bound to be in there somewhere. But ten minutes with Marie Louise would tell me whether she had really wanted to see me again or not, so about that not even Audrey would be telling a lie.

"Tell you what I'll do," I said. "Before I leave, I'll drop a note at the desk for Marie Louise, telling her I dropped by and was disappointed not to find her in—does she know you asked me for a cocktail?"

"No. And I'll get the glasses out of the way."

"—and that I'll call her later to make a date for an evening soon. We'll go to dinner and I'll take her to a place I know where there's a good singer—place called The Flea Club."

It was a low blow, and it worked. I really caught her off base. "The Flea Club!" she cried out, her voice taking things into its own hands for a change. Then she controlled herself and said more quietly, "Goodness, Hoop, do you really think, for a young girl, that is..."

"Have you ever been there?"

She lied spontaneously, "No, I haven't," and then immediately knew that a lie was foolish. "What am I talking about?" she said with a kind of laugh. "I mean, yes, I have."

"I wasn't thinking of taking her downstairs," I said, "although I'm a member. Maybe I will, at that. If my job is to keep her diverted, I might as well divert her all the way."

"I suppose it wouldn't really hurt her," Audrey said uneasily. "I'll just have to trust you." She rose. "You'll leave that note for her downstairs, won't you? I'm rather tired now and I have to pick her up at that movie. I think you've been awfully obliging."

"A pleasure, Mrs. Bellen," I said, and she took me to the door.

She took hold of the knob, turned it, and opened the door a couple of inches. Then she pushed it shut, released the knob, and turned her back to the door, as if to bar me from going out.

"Hoop. Wait."

She looked like somebody about to go off the high dive who had never gone off more than the edge of the bank before. Her eyes were wide and a little glassy. This was exactly the time for me to stop being even a spectator and to get out of there. I knew it; I felt a slight chilly contraction along my spine that told me she was going to do something worse than she had done yet. But I did just what she told me to. I waited.

Audrey said in a tight hard voice, "You said you were a direct type boy."

"Yes."

"All right, I'm going to be direct with you."

She pressed her hands together for a moment, then with an obvious effort of will separated them, letting one fall to her side, but the fingers of the other began fiddling at the neckline of her dress. Then, catching herself up again, she lowered that hand too, gave one more short little laugh, and said, "I don't want you to take Marie Louise out just once or twice. I want you to make a—a real campaign out of it."

And then, when I didn't answer—I didn't know what to answer—she said with a kind of agonised intensity, "I've got so little time left!"

She broke her eyes away from mine, put her hand to her forehead for a moment, pressing the fingers hard against the temples, even shook her head as if to clear it, and then looking at me again she said somewhat more calmly, "I can't help it if it sounds a little crazy. You're the first man Marie Louise has responded to since we began this dreadful trip, and—listen, I'm begging you. She's pretty, she's really the sweetest kind of child, I've—maybe exaggerated a little bit in the things I've told you about her nervous state, and she—"

She seemed to have come to the end of her rope, but then she blurted out, "Hoop, we could arrange things together. I'd make it worth your while."

I had been aware for minutes that there comes a point when your curiosity as a spectator reaches its limits of decency, and I knew now that I was in danger of going beyond it. Whatever Audrey was going to offer, I knew I didn't want any part of it.

"What," I thought, "exactly what in God's name is she driving at? For some utterly crazy reason is she asking me to seduce the girl? Marry her? Just show her around?—no, that wouldn't be anything to get all wound up about." But whatever it was, the thing she wanted to tell me, and hadn't been able to tell me because she couldn't bring herself to put it baldly and flatly and shockingly, was that this campaign involved Audrey and me in some kind of mutually profitable conspiracy at Marie Louise's expense.

That was the moment to shut her up, to get out of there and be rid of the whole thing. To this moment I'm not sure whether I let her go on to satisfy a morbid curiosity, or whether—as I like to tell myself —I knew that she was about to put me into a position where I would be able to protect Marie Louise, and that if I didn't, God knew what kind of villain she might dig up to make this proposition to, whatever the proposition was going to be.

I said deliberately, "What's in it for me?"

And it was exactly the right thing. She stood there stock still, then I could see her relax. Suddenly she was like an exhausted swimmer who finds he can touch bottom after all.

"That's just it," she said. "That's very sensible, a very sensible question. There could be a great deal in it for you, a very great deal. It's a practical world we live in after all, isn't it, Hoop? At your age you're not likely to fall romantically in love again—if you ever have been. If you married Marie Louise—I told you I was going to be direct, didn't I?—if you married Marie Louise, together we could—"

She stopped, abandoned whatever she was about to say, and continued, "Think about this, Hoop. See Marie Louise again as soon as you can. I'll do everything—everything I can to push things along, and we'll talk again. And please try to understand. Believe me, this situation is just as fantastic to me as it must be to you. I've been so desperately concerned, and this does look so much like—so much like a solution that—that might work out well for everyone."

"We'll see how things go," I said, because I had to say something.

"That's all I ask," Audrey said, "just that you give it a chance." She moved aside now and opened the door. Perhaps it was because the tiny hall had closed us in so privately, and now the door was open on to a public space. At any rate she shifted again, away from the odd, intense and revealing person she had been for a few minutes, back into something more like her old artificial self.

"Well, it's been quite an unusual afternoon, hasn't it?" she said. She extended her hand and I took it, and she turned her head just a little so that she had to look out at me from the corners of her eyes. Not too effective. "You've been a dear," she said, which was not at all what I would call what I had been, and withdrawing her hand, she closed the door and left me standing there.

"So have you," I said to nothing. "An absolute honey."

Downstairs, at the desk, I asked for an envelope and paper, and stood trying to decide just what to say to Marie Louise. I saw the switchboard light to 6-B flash on. I had just left 6-B. The operator listened to what 6-B asked for, and dialled the number. I was certain I caught the initials of the exchange, and I thought I caught the number too. It wasn't one I recognised, but I had a hunch.

Just in case I was guessing right, I asked to see the telephone directory for a minute.

And sure enough, Audrey had gone right to the phone to call René.

I finished the note to Marie Louise, and on my way home I entertained myself by imagining some of the conversations Audrey might have just had on the telephone with René. There was the one that went:

"Darling?...Audrey. Listen, darling, d'you know a man around The Flea Club named Hooper Taliaferro?...Oh, no, darling, I wouldn't call him that, in fact I think he's rather sweet in his way. Ordinary, of course, but rather sweet all the same...Well, no matter. Listen, darling, he's the one I palmed Marie Louise off on last night so we could be together. I told you...Yes, the same one, I'm certain of it, there couldn't be two with that name and both members of The Flea Club. And darling—now listen carefully, darling, I've managed it again for another night very soon, but there's a hitch...Well, I do my best, darling! well, I'm sorry!...Well, it's just that he might possibly take Marie Louise to The Flea Club, mightn't he, so hadn't we better plan to meet somewhere else?...*No*, dear, of *course* I don't care if he knows, but I'd hate for Marie Louise to find out until we..."

And the one that went:

"René?...Darling, it's Audrey. I called about the cheese. I was horrified when I found it in my purse!...Yes, this afternoon! I thought I had deposited it for you days ago...Yes, darling, twenty thousand. I hope you didn't run short in the meantime...But of *course* not, darling, not for a minute, I *love* to!...But no, darling, you mustn't say things like that...but of *course* I do, darling, you *know* I do...Oh, darling, I...but...but *na*turally, darling, *any*thing, all you have to do is to ask it... oh...oh, yes, I see...but...well, all right then, forty thousand."

I sort of liked that one. Then there was one that went:

"Darling, I've waited and waited for your call. What's the matter? Is anything wrong? Have I done something? I've been going crazy. Why haven't you..."

Then there was a short one that went:

"Darling, I just called to say I love you. I love you I love you I love you I love you..."

That was a sad one. By the time I got home, I was about ready to cry.

CHAPTER EIGHT

MARY FINNEY LISTENED to my account of Audrey's unusual proposition, sitting placidly and looking content indeed, in my most comfortable chair, with her feet propped up on my next-to-most comfortable chair. She was relaxed and happy, I could tell, and I suspected that at some time during my narrative she had surreptitiously loosened a couple of stays or some other kind of confining device, because she gave the impression of a slight but continuous spreading out and settling down, as she sat and listened.

When I stopped she said nothing, but continued to contemplate her toes, moving the big ones in a pair of reverse circles, at different speeds, experimentally.

Finally she said, "You called Audrey shrewd, once."

"Shrewd or calculating or something of the kind."

"She gave you that impression when you first met her."

"That's right."

"She sounds mighty naïve to me."

"Naïve?"

"Innocent as a lamb."

"Audrey does?"

"Yes. This last bit, out in the hallway. She sounds to me naïve, scared, floundering and desperate. Especially floundering. What did she mean, when she told you she had 'so little time left'?"

"Oh—getting old or something. Wanted to get rid of Marie Louise so she could have one last fling. Something like that."

"If that's all she wants, she could just let the girl go to hell. Wouldn't have to marry her off."

"Oh, come now. After all, she's her mother."

Dr. Finney grunted enigmatically. "You didn't get the impression, for instance, that she was working against a more definite deadline—something she had to get done in a few days, or weeks, or something like that?"

"No, I didn't. I didn't even think of it that way. Could be, I guess."

"And when she said it, she was looking, you might say, none too happy?"

"She was staring straight into a little corner of hell with her name on it," I said.

"Pretty bad, was it?"

"Terrible. You know they have this special section down in hell reserved for women like Audrey. It's lined with special mirrors and everywhere they look they see their faces enlarged so every pore and wrinkle looks like something on a relief map of the Grand Canyon. Their hair is always falling out and every time they reach for their lipsticks they find they've lost them somewhere. The imps in charge are beautiful young men but they don't use pitchforks or anything, they just stand around talking to other imps disguised as beautiful young girls, and now and then one of them glances over at all the Audreys and says, 'Look at that hideous old hag over there.' It's one of the worst spots in the whole place."

Dr. Finney looked at me suspiciously. "My heart's bleeding," she said. "Where'd you pick up that stuff?"

"I've always known about it," I said. "I thought everybody did."

"Sure," said Dr. Finney. "Now—did you make another date with Marie Louise?"

"I did."

"Tell me about it. I'll make the coffee this time."

She got up and began puttering around with the alcohol lamp. "You know, Hoopy," she said, giving me a nice grin indeed, "I'm having a hell of a good time."

I called Marie Louise only a few hours after that talk with Audrey, and asked her if she could go to dinner with me the next day.

"I'd love to," she said, and her voice was actually friendly.

There just wasn't any point in going into her big change of heart, over the phone. The gap was too big. So all I said was "Good."

"For that matter," said Marie Louise, "I'm not busy tonight, and I've already eaten and I'm all dressed, if you want to come around and go somewhere. Some club or something?" She was being casual, very very casual.

I had absolutely nothing to do that night, and am not ordinarily much of a teaser, but with an advantage like this one I had to follow it through. "Gosh, I'm sorry, I'm busy," trying to suggest a bevy of ballerinas, all begging to drink champagne out of my slippers. "It'll have to be Monday. Is there any particular place you'd like to eat?"

"This place you mentioned the other night," she said. "What was the name of it? A club or something," and boy, she was a poor dissembler. She had a passionate interest in The Flea Club all of a sudden and she was trying to sound casual about it but the effect was about as casual as a ham actress involved in a big scene from *Medea*.

"The name of it was The Flea Club," I told her, "and at the time, you said that if you'd ever heard of a place with a name like The Flea Club you couldn't have forgotten it."

She said awkwardly, "Well—yes, that was it, The Flea Club. Could we eat there?"

"No."

"Oh, Hoop!" she wailed, in real distress. "Why not?"

"Because they don't serve meals, Marie Louise. Anyway, nothing goes on there until ten o'clock at the earliest. If you think you can hold out that long, I'll come around at eight and we'll eat somewhere, and then I'll take you to The Flea Club. All right?"

"Perfect," she said, and then a little hesitantly, but picking up as she went along. "Look, I'm sorry I was so soggy. You're nice to ask me again."

"Think nothing of it. See you tomorrow."

"I'll be looking forward to it."

"Me too. So long."

"So long. And thanks—really."

❀❀❀

It wasn't half an hour before Audrey called me. "Hoop—I'm so pleased."

"That's good."

"I haven't long. I have to get back upstairs. There's no one with Marie Louise and I don't want to leave her alone. I want to ask you another favour."

"Go ahead."

"I've some friends who've turned up unexpectedly and we'll probably be out quite late Monday night. Can you give me any idea how long you'll have Marie Louise out?"

"You mean you want me to keep her out late," I said. I did not say, "So that you can have that much more time with René."

"Well, yes, to be frank."

"All right. I'll keep her out until two at least. No guarantee beyond that."

"Oh—Well, thanks, Hoop. Thanks so much. You're a darling, really. Call me Tuesday and we'll get together and you must tell me everything. I'm hoping for so much!"

I couldn't help hoping for a little something myself, but not anything like what Audrey had in mind. All I wanted was a pleasant evening with a pretty girl who interested me more than I could figure out any good reason for. But it was apparent from the minute Marie Louise came down to the lobby that nothing was going to happen. She was polite. She was even friendly. Oddly enough, she seemed excited. But she wasn't excited about me. Along about the middle of dinner, over the second half of a steak, I decided that the world was full of plenty of things good enough that I didn't have to feel bad because Marie Louise and I weren't striking sparks off one another, pleasant as that would have been.

So I stopped whatever small talk we were making and said: "Listen, child. You've got me feeling like your great-uncle. I'm willing to settle for that, but I want to know what made you decide all of a sudden why you were so eager to go out with me again. I telephone you and I hear you in the background telling your mother that you won't you won't you won't and you won't go out with me again."

"But you called again, all the same."

"Yes, I called again, but I suppose you know why. You must know that this is a command performance."

It took her a moment to accept this, then she said evenly, "I hoped against hope you really called back of your own accord. Mother swore you did. But I suppose—did Mother—"

"Yes, Mother did, and here we are. Now shoot straight with Uncle Hooper and tell me why we're here—from your point of view, that is."

"All right," she said, and I liked the way she stopped pretending. "We're here because I've just got to go to The Flea Club and I didn't know anyone else who could take me."

"Sure. The Flea Club. The one you couldn't even remember the name of."

"Of course I remembered it."

"You claimed you forgot it."

"I know I did. That was just silly of me. I was trying to take advantage of you, and when I try to take advantage of somebody I get embarrassed about it and do something silly like that."

"Marie Louise, I'm going to fall in love with you yet. Now let's see where we are: you were suddenly just crazy to go to The Flea Club, which you hadn't even heard of Saturday night, and you remembered I'd mentioned it, so you decided you had to go out with me again in order to get in. Is that right so far?"

She gulped and said, "Yes, that's right. I'm awful."

"On the contrary. You're delightful. Let me get this straight: when Audrey talked to me she said you had decided I was pretty nice. The phrase 'taking quite a shine' to me was used."

"I didn't use it! " she said indignantly, and then tried to soften it with, "But you're really nice. I didn't realise it until tonight."

"In an uncle-ish sort of way I get by. Look, I'm not hurt, I'm just terribly terribly curious. Will you please for Pete's sake tell me what's this sudden passion for The Flea Club?"

She took a deep breath as if she were going to do the next fifty yards under water, then blurted out, "It's about Nicole."

I waited.

"I'm just fascinated by her."

I waited some more.

"And I want to meet her."

It had worked twice. I waited again.

"That's all."

I said, "Nicole's a grand person and I can introduce you. But you're not fascinated by her, because you'd never heard tell of her until yesterday."

"I had so!"

"You'd never even heard of The Flea Club until I mentioned it."

"Well what difference does that make? My goodness, I've got all Nicole's records, every one. I just didn't know she was at The Flea Club, that's all. My goodness, it doesn't say anything about it on her records!"

"That's true. How did you learn she was there?"

She hesitated on this one, then said, "I read it in a paper while I was having my chocolate."

"Pooh. The Flea Club doesn't advertise. It's a membership proposition."

"I know it is. This was in some write-up or other. Sort of a round-about-the-town thing."

"Ma-rie Lou-ise…"

"Well, it was!"

"What was the name of the paper?"

"I don't remember! Some little old paper or other. You're giving me such a quiz!"

"Hm. Well, one more question, if you've got all her records. What's the name of her accompanist and composer?"

"How should I know? Are they the same?"

"Usually. Now think."

She sat there with her brows knit. Audrey had knit hers for me, and added five years to her age. Marie Louise looked about twelve.

Suddenly her whole face lit up and she cried out so loud that the people at the next table jumped and looked at us. "Groute! Antoine Groute! No—Croute!"

"Bingo! But you haven't got all her records, just her early ones. He's changed it to Tony Crew."

"Anyway, I win, don't I? You'll take me now, won't you? You'll introduce me to Nicole?"

"And Tony Crew, on the chance that he's the one you're fascinated by."

I told myself she was lying somewhere. After all, she was Audrey's daughter. But she was very young and very pretty, which, I decided, made it just innocent fibbing. Entirely different thing altogether. Sort of charming, when you came right down to it.

Although I went to The Flea Club two or three times a week, even if only for a short nightcap, and occasionally had to take a guest, I had never before turned up with anyone who was unusual in any way. They would be people from home who had looked me up, or friends of people like my female cousin, that I couldn't get out of looking up. They were always nice enough but never of any particular distinction. Just people. So my appearance with a pretty young girl was something of a sensation, in a small kind of way, with the people who knew me around there.

Marie Louise was really looking extremely pretty, and also she was looking extremely young and fresh in an assemblage where even the best-looking women usually looked jaded. She looked brand-new, whereas everybody else bore at least the first visible symptoms of ultimate dissolution, and her excitement looked young and natural whereas the typical Flea Club habituée, even if she had an excited look, owed it to alcohol or some less innocent stimulation.

Bibi came up to Marie Louise and looked at her as if she were looking into some extraordinary and disturbing mirror. The two girls were about of a height, and of more or less the same general colouring and build. There wasn't even too much difference between their features, if you wanted to force the comparison, but even so, they might have come from different planets. Bibi's eyes travelled over Marie Louise from hair to shoes, and then, curiously, she stepped up and took a bit of the material of Marie Louise's dress between her fingers and rubbed it, as a shopper might do in a store, as if she were trying to explain to herself the difference between what she was and what Marie Louise was, on some less terrifying level than the obvious one. During all this examination Marie Louise stood quite still, uncertain and I think a little frightened, glancing at me in a puzzled and questioning way for some kind of help. I said, "Bibi, meet Marie Louise," but Bibi said nothing. She dropped the fold of the dress and turned and walked away, taking up her position at the end of the bar.

Freddy Fayerweather came bouncing up and said, "My dear! How refreshing! A sweet pea in a patch of deadly nightshade! Do introduce me!"

"Marie Louise—" (avoiding "Miss Bellen" in case anybody around there knew Audrey's last name) "—meet Freddy. Mr. Gratzhaufer of St. Paul."

"*Hoop*ee," shrieked Freddy. "*Ra*ley! My name's Fayerweather, Miss—Marie Louise—or anyway it *prac*tically is. Now tell me about yourself."

"Well..." said Marie Louise, and stopped.

"Where's Tony, Freddy? I want him to meet Marie Louise. She knows his records."

"No! Really? But she's a *what*cha-ma-callit. A cogno*scent*e! He's back with Nicole. Why don't you two come sit at my table?"

Marie Louise was looking at Freddy the way she might have at some monster that had suddenly grown legs and walked out of an aquarium tank. And come to think of it, Freddy's features, with their soft and slightly blurred quality, were like something seen through water. But she made no objection, so we went over to his table to wait for Nicole's number.

Freddy prattled along, telling Marie Louise about Tony's virtues and hinting at everyone else's shortcomings, trying to find out what was what between Marie Louise and me, and generally skittering around in his own little world of intrigue, frustration, and false excitement, and in the middle of all this I caught sight of the Italian boy, over at the bar. Bibi was just leaving him, probably having found he wasn't ticklish, and his eyes were searching the room. When he saw me, his face lit up with recognition, and he made a bee-line for our table. Nobody would have called him a sweet pea in a patch of deadly nightshade but he was the male counterpart of Marie Louise—a very nice fresh-looking kid.

"Howdy," I said. "How did you get in?"

He showed me the card I had given him the other night. "Nobody asked for it," he said, "so I kept it. Nobody asked for it tonight, either."

"I guess you look honest. Uh—afraid I don't know your name."

"Balducci, Luigi Balducci."

"Uh—Marie Louise, Luigi Balducci. Luigi, Freddy Fayerweather. Have a seat." It wasn't exactly according to the etiquette book but for The Flea Club it was almost stuffy. Also it was Freddy's table and I had no right to ask the boy to sit there, especially since it left no place free for Tony to join us later, but he so obviously wanted to be asked, and Marie Louise was so close to being foundered in the wash of Freddy's chatter, that I was glad to take on Luigi as a stabilising element.

I have always said I don't believe in love at first sight, and I still say it. People think it happens, but it happens in retrospect, not really at first sight. But I must admit that what hadn't happened between Marie Louise and me I could see happening between her and Luigi. It wasn't sparks, but I swear there was something like a flow of light between them. That sounds a little sloppy. All I mean is, something happened. It was like watching one of those magician's tricks, where he takes an empty flower-pot, pours water in it, and a great big son-of-a-bitch of a geranium begins to grow and unfold into leaf and blossom before your eyes. It was so obvious that even Freddy noticed it. "Well *Hoop*," he said, highly pleased, not at what was happening but at my possible discomfiture, "if you had anything in *mind*, I mean if you had any *plans* or de*signs*, I think you've made an irre*triev*able mistake! "

The lights went down and Tony and Nicole came in for their number. The turn went pretty well, probably to Freddy's disappointment, and in due time Tony and Nicole took their applause and Nicole began to move about from table to table. But Tony neither went with her—which was not unusual—nor came over to Freddy's table—which was. He went instead down the stairway to the cellar.

Freddy went through a miniature gamut of emotions, ranging from ordinary surprise through alarm to extreme fidgetiness—if fidgetiness can be an emotion. It could be, with Freddy. He gave me a huffy little glare—he was really at his worst—and said, "Well, if you *will* fill my table for me!" and it was true that there was no chair now for Tony, with Luigi there, but it was also true that Tony had headed for the stairway without even looking in our direction. "I'll simply have to go find him," Freddy said, getting up. "'Scuse."

"Bring him back, Marie Louise wants to meet him," I said. "We'll pull up another chair."

Freddy vanished, and shortly Nicole reached our table. I introduced Luigi and Marie Louise and told Nicole why we were there—or at any rate told her Marie Louise's story about why we were there. Nicole was pleased, and responsive to both of them, and sat down in Freddy's chair, motioning to the barman that he could bring her usual lemon soda to that table.

Marie Louise said something about how lovely the number had been.

"You liked it? I'm glad. But it was not a very happy one, was it? I tell you what I will do. The next one I sing will be a happy one, and I will sing it especially for you and your husband. It is about honeymooners." Nicole smiled at both of them, but seeing their expression, added, "It *is* your honeymoon, of course?"

Marie Louise and Luigi made odd sounds together, among which it was possible to isolate a few phrases such as, "Well, yes, or rather, why no, that is, we're not married but it is true that we just met," the general sense being, by implication, that the world had begun about thirty minutes ago.

"Just met?" said Nicole incredulously. "Absurd."

"But true," I said. "I just introduced them. But I see exactly what you mean. Nicole, will you hold this place? I want to get Tony for Marie Louise."

I let myself into the cellar stairway with my key, descended the stairs, turned the corner into the members' room, and saw it occupied by only three people at one table, but it was as unexpected a trio as I could have named—Freddy, Tony and Mrs. Jones. Over in one corner gaped the two pits of Professor Johnson's excavations.

Freddy was pink with agitation, Tony's lips were set in a firm line less suggestive of his typical gentle patience than usual, and Mrs. Jones seemed on the point of tears.

"Good evening," I said to everybody.

"Honestly, Hoop, you're in the way everywhere tonight," Freddy complained. "Every time I turn round, you're in my hair. Hattie, dear, you know Hoop Taliaferro?"

Mrs. Jones nodded as if we had never seen one another and so did I, and I said, "Tony, there's a girl upstairs would like to meet you if you have a minute before you go on again?"

Freddy said, "Can't you see we're in*volved*? Go away."

Mrs. Jones said, with a tremble in her voice, "Why should he go away? Everybody knows all my private affairs. All they have to do is look in the newspapers." She began to cry, in a small habitual way that didn't interfere too much with her other activities. These included a large glass of whisky and soda.

"Well, if you want to make public enter*tain*ment out of it," Freddy said.

Mrs. Jones cried harder, murmured, "...humiliating..." and then reached out suddenly and put her hand over Tony's where it rested on the table. She remained clutching it, wiping her eyes with her other hand. "Oh, T-T-Tony," she whimpered, and then, forced to abandon either Tony's hand or her handkerchief in order to lift up her glass, she stopped crying and put away the handkerchief and took a long drink. She seemed to improve immediately.

I said, "I'd better get along. I'd appreciate it if you can stop by on your way up, Tony. I hope you feel better, Mrs. Jones. So long, Freddy," and I turned to go.

"Don't leave," Mrs. Jones said. "Why leave? Freddy, I wish *you'd* leave. Sit down, Harper," she said, and I didn't bother to correct her. "I haven't any pride. Why should I have any pride? But one thing I never thought I'd find myself doing, I never thought I'd find myself in a position like this. Tell him what I did, Tony. I don't think it was so awful."

Freddy volunteered, "She just tried to buy Tony right out from under me, that's all."

The merchandise under discussion got an even grimmer look on his face, but didn't move or say anything.

"And I simply refuse to allow it," Freddy went on in a righteous tone. "It's simply too absolutely de*grad*ing for wor—"

"*Tony!*" wailed Mrs. Jones. Tony had jumped up, which jerked his hand out from under hers. He started striding across the room, and went up the stairs fast, and disappeared.

"Tony!" the poor thing wailed again, "Tony, don't leave me! Oh, Tony, I love you!" but he was gone, and she put both hands in front of her face and made unlovely burbly noises. She had had a lot more to drink than I thought.

Freddy said, "Well, really, Hattie, if you *will* put yourself into these *ter*rible positions, I don't see how you can expect to get anything but *hurt*."

She mumbled, damply and thickly, "He's so wonderful."

Freddy emitted something divided between a laugh and a jeer and a gasp, and said to me, "You know what I want for Tony, Hoop, I've told you. I want to protect him from just this kind of thing. And I come down here looking for him and what do I find? Hattie, of all people! And now, of all times!" He turned to poor Mrs. Jones and said, "Honestly, Hattie, pride or no pride, I should think you'd realise that a boy like Tony wouldn't look twice at you, especially when his first look, so to speak, was like the other night. And anyway he's mine, and I don't mean that the way you think I do, either, if you're getting nasty-minded about it. So—"

"He's not!" Mrs. Jones cried out, taking down her hands and giving one good strong wipe at her eyes. "You just bother the life out of him, that's all. You just pester him! He doesn't like you one bit!"

Freddy's laugh tried to be contemptuous, but there were uncertain overtones in it. "Now I know you're crazy," he said. "Who told you that?"

"He did!" said Mrs. Jones. "Just now!"

Freddy's face turned into shrimp-coloured blubber and began to vibrate. "I don't believe it," he said, "I simply don't believe it and I won't accept it. I'll tell Tony what you said."

But he did believe it, he knew it was true, whether Tony had actually said it or not, and I saw he was going to cry. I didn't want to see it, and for that matter I didn't want to see anything that was going to happen from then on. I got out faster than Tony had.

In her time, Mrs. Jones had experienced the birth of love in lots of different ways, I imagined. But that it should come while she was pinioned in the arms of a handsome boy, while she kicked and screamed and fought in hysterics, was something entirely new, I suspected, and probably as sudden and as lively as the most jaded could ask. Eros, as was usual around The Flea Club, was working overtime at strange ways in which his wonders to perform. And this one was really novel all the way through, since for the first time, Mrs. Jones seemed to have fallen in love with an un-son-of-a-bitch.

All of this was happening the night before the murder.

CHAPTER NINE

"WE HAVE NOW arrived," said Dr. Finney, "at the point where you went back upstairs and found Marie Louise had skipped out on you with the Italian boy."

"We've arrived at the point where I'm going to have a couple of hours sleep. I'm full of fatigue poisons."

"It's 5.30. Give me another half-hour and then I'll give you until 8.00. Now tell me about Marie Louise."

"She did not skip out on me. When I came upstairs she and Luigi and Nicole were talking like old friends together, very animated and all. No sign of Tony."

"Any idea where he went or what he was doing?"

"None. Is it important?"

"How do I know? At this stage, everything's important. Go ahead."

"I joined them at the table and Nicole told me she thought my young friends were charming. Came time for her second number and she left us and pretty soon came out on the stage, etcetera. Tony seemed O.K. Nicole sang like a million bucks, got a terrific hand. Had to do a couple of encores. Came back to our table and Marie Louise said she was thrilled, which she obviously was, you could see it. Said she had to go home, though, and would I mind taking her. It was only a little after twelve, and I remembered what I had said to Audrey about keeping Marie Louise out late, but I didn't regard it as a contract. Asked Marie Louise to wait while I made a phone call. Called their suite at the Prince du Royaume. No answer. If Audrey and René were there, I didn't want Marie Louise bumping into anything bothersome. They must have been at René's."

"Taking it for granted they were together."

"Taking that for granted, yes. So I went back to the table—Nicole was still there—and said to Marie Louise, 'O.K., let's go.' The Italian boy said why didn't I just stay there and he would take Marie Louise home and then come back and join us. I said I thought that was a lousy idea and he apologised. So Nicole said was I coming back, and I said no, it was late and I thought I'd go on home. Where Tony was, all this time, I don't know. Luigi asked if it was all right if he stayed on, was he wearing out his welcome considering he wasn't a member or anything, and Nicole said of course not, he was welcome to stay as her guest, and please do. He said he'd love to. I took Marie Louise home. Kissed her good-night. Turned out to be avuncular in the extreme. She said thank you, said she wanted to thank me a thousand times for a thrilling evening, she had never met anyone quite as wonderful as Nicole, good-night, Hoop. I went home. End of day."

"Sleep well?"

"Like a top."

"So the next morning you called for Emmy and me—I guess we have to call that 'yesterday morning' now—and I should know everything from that time on. But you're hiding something from me. Aren't you?"

"I have been."

"Ready to talk?"

"I can really have a couple of hours sleep afterwards?"

"Sure. Promise."

"I'll talk. Here goes."

I will first fill in for the record, as briefly as possible, that I called for Dr. Finney and Emmy late. It was about 8:45, but I had said eight o'clock breakfast. I had called Professor Johnson, in spite of the hour, from my place, but hadn't had an answer. I called him twice from Dr. Finney's suite, once when I arrived, and then after breakfast. That time, at nearly ten, I got him. I told him I had a couple of friends who would be really interested if he had time to explain the excavations in the basement of The Flea Club, and he said if I could give him half an hour he could meet us there. So Dr. Finney and Emmy and I went to St. Julien-le-Pauvre first after all, thus compounding a minor violation of chronological sequence, and thence proceeded to the members' entrance of The Flea Club. Since we were punctual people and Professor Johnson a punctual person, we met there, and went in together.

I won't try to be dramatic about it. It was a horrible shock and no fun to remember. Although it was now mid-morning, the cellar was still a mess from last night. A few tables had been cleaned up; the rest were still littered with glasses and ashes. Professor Johnson, a fastidious man, looked with distaste at the room, and began pointing out vestigial indications along the walls of the original chapel structure. He had had trouble getting permission to begin the excavations. Nicole had objected, and he had had to get an injunction, or whatever it is called, from the *Monuments Historiques*. It had turned out very well, since the excavations, in spite of the mess, were an odd fillip for a night-club cellar, and everybody enjoyed them. Professor Johnson was digging up the entire area, small sections at a time, to a depth of eight feet, hunting indications of the original floor and so on. Then these holes would be filled in, and adjacent areas explored. The two pits now in the club were due to be filled that day, and he was commenting that we were fortunate to have hit just that time, when we discovered that one of the pits was more than half filled, and that a figure was lying in it half covered with earth. It didn't make any sense to me at all when I first saw it. It was like rags. Flesh was showing too, but I suppose I just refused to recognise it. Then it wasn't rags, it was Nicole's robe, and the flesh was her neck and head and part of one arm, everything in twisted and unnatural positions.

Let me just put it this way: we managed to get her out. The wound on her head was sticky and clogged with earth. In no time Emmy had appeared with water and a wet bar cloth, and Dr. Finney was washing and exploring the wound, and saying, "Hoop, somebody just left here. This is fresh. You two men go look through the place. Hurry up. And take something along to hit somebody with if you find him."

I grabbed a shovel, and so did Professor Johnson, and we went up to the bar floor. We looked into the washrooms and behind the bar and behind the stage and that was all there was to it. Then we started upstairs and I said, "We're crazy. He might still be in the basement. He might kill them."

"I'll go," Professor Johnson said. "You go on up. Call if you need me."

It wasn't my kind of business and I wasn't happy at it. With Professor Johnson gone everything seemed awfully quiet. I knew there wasn't much chance I would find anybody. If somebody had been there when we came, which was obvious, since they had been interrupted in filling the pit, they had only to run up the cellar stairs and out the boulevard door which operated on a spring lock. But I kept a tight hold on my shovel all the same. The door to Nicole's living-room was open. I peered in. The furniture returned my look incuriously. The door to the bedroom was closed. I turned the knob without making any noise at all, waited to get the feel of it, and then pushed it open suddenly.

There they were, the Italian boy and Marie Louise. The room was full of a warmish glow, with the pale morning sun cutting through the slats of the shutters on one wall, and the heater making a red live spot near the bed. They were as pretty as anything I ever expect to see, Marie Louise the colour of the inside of a shell, and Luigi as brown as if he were sunburned all over, both of them against the rumpled white of the sheet. They were beautifully and wonderfully asleep. It was a shame to have to back up and close that door, but I did. Then I knocked on it, hard.

Silence.

Then a stirring and a kind of whispering and mumbling. Then Luigi's voice, a little thick and deepened.

"Nicole?" he said doubtfully. I hadn't knocked in a lady-like manner.

"It's not Nicole, it's Hooper Taliaferro."

No answer, but I could imagine that the silence was full of alarm on the other side of the door. "Hooper Taliaferro," I repeated. "Friend." I hated the thought of all the sudden waking excitement and scare I must be throwing them into. "Wake up and open up."

Sounds of agitation. Mattress-and-springs sounds, and footsteps, a kind of scampering, which had to be Marie Louise making for shelter.

Luigi: "Wait a minute."

"I'm sorry, this is urgent. Get dressed and leave here in a hurry. Don't stop for nothing."

Agitated whispers and rustlings. "Just a minute."

The door opened and Luigi stood there, barefoot, his hair every which way all over his head, in shirt and pants, still fastening his belt.

"Nicole isn't here," he said, "I don't want you to think I've been with Nicole. Just because I—"

"I know you haven't been with Nicole. Shut up and listen. There's been a terrible accident downstairs and the police will be here. People are in the cellar. If you hurry maybe you can get out the door on to the boulevard." I raised my voice and called out into space, "You too, Marie Louise."

There was a small shriek from behind a closed door beyond the bed—the bathroom probably. The door opened part way and Marie Louise's head appeared round its edge. "For goodness' sake," she said, "how did you know I was here? Did—" and then as if she guessed, her eyes widened and she gave another small shriek and closed the door.

"Never mind. Just hurry."

Luigi had been getting into his socks and shoes. He tied the laces and jumped up, found his necktie lying on the floor, picked it up, and began tying it. By the time he had got into his coat, Marie Louise came out of the bathroom, all dressed and running a comb through her hair. She had on a street dress, not the fancy dress I had left her in not very many hours before at the Prince du Royaume. Her face was about as red as faces get, and she was saying, "Now you listen to me, Hooper Taliaferro—"

"You're listening, I'm talking," I said. "You've got to get out of here. Incidentally where does Audrey think you are? With me?"

She said something just as much beside the point, considering what the situation was, "What's that shovel for?"

"Protection," I said, and let her wonder. "The hell with it. Nicole's been badly hurt, downstairs. There's a doctor there now and there'll be police if they aren't there already. I've got to get right down there. The two of you, get out of here by the boulevard door right away. Don't leave anything behind. When you go out on the street, just do it naturally and hope you won't be noticed in the crowd. Don't let anybody know you were here, under any circumstances, or you'll be involved in a nasty investigation. Also it'll come out that you spent the night together, if that makes any difference to you. It doesn't to me. Personally, I congratulate the two of you. Now I'm leaving. I'll keep anybody from coming upstairs, somehow, if I can, for the next few minutes. Keep your mouths shut—or lie, but you weren't here. See? Now get out."

I went down to stave people off the cellar stair. The last I saw of Marie Louise and Luigi, they were just standing there with their mouths open.

When I got back to the cellar, a police ambulance was outside and Nicole was being carried out. I asked Mary Finney, "Is she dead?"

"She's alive," Dr. Finney said. "Beyond that, I can't tell."

"Was she conscious? Did she say anything?"

"She said something," said Dr. Finney. "It sounded like '*gutzeit*.'"

❀❀❀

And so, having confessed to Dr. Finney, I had brought things up to date. Through my windows we could see the first suggestion of chilly grey light in the street. Dr. Finney heaved a great sigh, lowered her feet, and began putting on her shoes.

"Exactly why didn't you want to tell me about Marie Louise and Luigi?" she asked.

"After all," I said.

"Oh, that," said Dr. Finney. "I respect your motives as a gentleman, but I deplore the hell out of your attitude as my co-sleuth. No other reason?"

"Also, the whole thing was too sweet and innocent to have anything to do with a murder. If you had seen them lying there—"

"I practically did, the way you gloated over it."

"They didn't have anything to do with what happened downstairs. I didn't see any reason why their night together should be contaminated by getting mixed up with any subsequent investigation."

"I'm inclined to think you're absolutely right, Hoopy. Inclined but not convinced. Now I'm going back to the hotel." She stood, making smoothing motions of adjustment here and there. "Here's the programme. It's almost six now. We'll have breakfast in that seraglio where I'm holed up—eight-thirty. First I want to talk to Marie Louise. That won't be hard to arrange, one way or another, I imagine. Then I've got to arrange somehow to talk to most of these other people you've mentioned. We'll just have to manage somehow. I figure we've got toe-holds on most of them, one way or another, but you'll have to help."

"Do what I can," I said. "Freddy's easy, of course. And Tony should be. I don't know about Mrs. Jones—"

"Anybody who can get Tony can get Mrs. Jones, I imagine."

"Probably. I'm not sure about René."

"Get him through Audrey."

"And get Audrey through me. All right, I suppose we can get everybody—if we can find them at home."

"We'll find them. We'll call before they have a chance to stagger out. From the sound of everything you've told me about them, they ought to be available until noon."

"All right. Do you think we can call again about Nicole now?"

I had called as often as she would let me, during the past eighteen hours. But, "Go ahead, if you'll rest easier," she said.

It didn't make me rest any easier, but I had been ready for the news. Nicole was dead.

CHAPTER TEN

A PAIR OF waiters, with the air of minor deities, were arranging a breakfast table in Dr. Finney's suite at the Prince du Royaume. As upon a sacrificial altar, they spread a celestially white cloth and four napkins folded into pyramids. The offerings came next—china, silver, baskets of *brioches* and *croissants*, jars of pale butter, urns of cream and sugar, pitchers of coffee and chocolate, and a great ornamental bowl full of fresh ripe apricots and cherries, garnished with grape leaves, flown from wherever apricots and cherries and grape leaves can be flown from to Paris in midwinter, to indicate that the whole business was really on an astral plane, removed from such limiting considerations as time, space, and the seasonal relationship between the earth and the sun, not to mention the vulgarity of money as anything but a convenient and inexhaustible medium of exchange.

The four of us—Mary Finney, Miss Collins, Marie Louise and myself—sat waiting to fall upon this fantasy and demolish it. When the waiters had pushed our chairs under us and left, Dr. Finney flipped her napkin open and said graciously, "Well, we might as well get busy and eat this stuff."

"Of course," she said a few minutes later to Marie Louise, "there's no reason why you should tell us what we want to know unless you want to."

It seemed to me that there was at least a friendly obligation, since I had discovered her and Luigi there and had let them get out without having to go through the police, but I didn't object, especially since Marie Louise answered, "Oh, but I do. I want to tell the whole thing. It'll be a relief—at last! There's no reason why I should feel funny about it. After all, it's only the truth."

"How old are you?" Dr. Finney asked. "Hoop thinks seventeen or eighteen."

"Seventeen!" she cried. "I've been eighteen for what seems like years and years, and I'll be nineteen in exactly five weeks. If I were only seventeen, I'd go absolutely crazy waiting."

"Waiting for what?"

"For nineteen. I'm going to tell you everything, absolutely everything, and I can't help how it sounds. I can't help how mean it sounds to Mama, or anything like that."

"Hooray," commented Dr. Finney.

"I wish I could say it all at once," Marie Louise said. "Well—in the first place, you know we're married."

Mary Finney said, "Naturally," at the same time that I said, "You and who?"

"*Who?*" cried Marie Louise. "Who do you think? Me and Luigi! My goodness, do you think I go to bed with every—"

"Naturally not."

I said to Mary Finney, "How long have you known about this?"

"From the time you told me about finding them in bed," she said. Emily Collins gave a violent start, but without explaining anything Dr. Finney went on, using two words not ordinarily current in missionary circles, even the most medical, "She's obviously neither bitch nor pushover."

"*Mary*!" breathed Miss Collins, and then, "What's a pushover?"

We explained, and I went back a few sentences and said to Marie Louise, "What do you mean, go crazy waiting? It doesn't seem to me that you've waited for anything much."

"Better begin at the beginning, if you can decide where that would be," said Dr. Finney.

"The beginning," Marie Louise said reflectively. "Well, that would be when I went off to school. Of course I had been in all these other places that were practically prisons they were so strict. But then my grandfather's will said Audrey could choose the schools until I was eighteen, but when I was eighteen I could choose my own school. So—"

"You called her 'Mama' a while ago and now you call her 'Audrey'," Dr. Finney interjected.

"That's what she likes me to call her, since Daddy died—Audrey. I don't like it. I think it's silly. Daddy always wanted me to call her Mama. Actually she's only my stepmother anyway, but I never knew my own mother, she died when I was only two years old, and Audrey's been around as long as I can remember. I guess mostly I call her Mama when she feels like my mother, and Audrey when she's just like—a governess or boss or something."

"I see. Excuse all these interruptions, but what about this grandfather's will? Where does all your money come from, yours and Audrey's, just to get to the root of everything?"

"I can't say everything at once, and eat too," said Marie Louise. "You see Daddy's dead. He died a long time ago. I was twelve. I guess he didn't amount to much, but he was awfully sweet. He never worked or anything. It was his money, not Audrey's. Rather, it was his father's—my grandfather's money, that is, mine now, or will be when I'm nineteen."

"Clearer and clearer," I murmured to myself, and then aloud, "Excuse me for asking, but has Audrey got any money at all?"

"Goodness no!" said Marie Louise as if it were one of the fundamental facts of life that everyone should know without asking. "For that matter, neither did Daddy. Grandfather let us have practically anything, but it was always his, not ours. Then Daddy died, and all his life long he'd never had a nickel except what Grandfather had given him, and four years ago Grandfather died, and I guess the will was sort of a shock to Audrey, when you come down to it."

She paused a moment, said, "Poor Audrey," in a not altogether compassionate tone, and then went on, "It's quite a lot of money. And it's all mine. Audrey gets an awfully big allowance, and so do I, except that she controls it. Until I'm nineteen. Then I get all the money and Audrey gets a little old dinky allowance—a hundred dollars a week, and that won't keep her in face cream. Well, I'll give her all of that old money she needs, but do you know—"

She stopped again, so long that Dr. Finney said, "Know what?"

"—I don't think she trusts me to give her enough. I think she feels sort of insecure about things. And then she's so afraid I won't marry the way she wants me to. She wants me to marry a prince or a duke or something, I think, or at least a rich man."

At this point Marie Louise smiled and added, "Well, I sure didn't. Luigi's father runs a grocery store. So what happened," she went on, "was that after I'd been to all these awful schools like prisons that Audrey sent me to, when I was eighteen and could choose I said I was going to college in New York. So there I went, I went to Sarah Lawrence. That was a mistake—not the school, I don't mean, but New York. I thought it would be the one place I'd be free at last, but Audrey had all these dozens of friends there and they kept pestering me and pestering me. It was all supposed to be so sweet and friendly and everything, but what they were really doing, they were checking up on me for Audrey all the time. Day and night, practically. I wouldn't be surprised if Audrey paid them."

"Phooey," I said. "Anybody can find a way to dodge people and get off alone in New York."

Marie Louise turned on me with spirit. "That's what you think," she said. "You just don't know what it is to be a young girl and timid and inexperienced. Of course it's different now," she said with satisfaction, looking back from the heights of worldliness, "and as a matter of fact I did learn towards the end of the year how to get out by myself. Otherwise how do you suppose I ever managed to marry Luigi?"

"I haven't the slightest idea. How'd you ever make contact with Luigi in the first place?"

"I walked into this little old grocery store," said Marie Louise, "and there he was."

"You mean like with a price tag and everything?"

"No, silly, behind the counter. Audrey had this friend down in the Village with an apartment, and she used to have me down to keep me guarded weekends. So once all these other awful old hags were in having cocktails and they ran out of soda, so I said I'd go out and get some. So I went into this little old grocery store and—" here Marie Louise almost melted—"and there was this beautiful little old Italian boy behind the counter. Luigi!"

"Of all people!" I said, but Dr. Finney scowled at me.

"So it wasn't a mistake coming to New York after all. And I bought half a dozen bottles of soda and told him I'd be at the Metropolitan Museum Sunday afternoon, at two o'clock, at the postcard stand."

"Just like that? You said give me half a dozen bottles of soda and meet me at the Museum?"

"Of course not," Marie Louise said patiently. "We talked a little while first."

"What about?"

"About us."

"But what did you have to say to each other?" I asked, really dumbfounded.

"Why, everything! " said Marie Louise. "What our names were, and how old we were, and what we were doing, and everything like that. We had plenty to talk about. It was his father's store, and Luigi was going to night school and saving to go to law school. He still is. Still going to, I mean. So that's what we talked about. All those things."

"And then?"

"Then we decided to get married."

"Right then and there?"

"No!" said Marie Louise. "Can't you understand anything at all? First we went to all these museums. Everybody thought it was wonderful, how interested I was in museums. Sometimes I'd have to be with some of these friends of Audrey's but they couldn't take the museums. They'd say they'd pick me up later, and Luigi would always be following us around until these friends of Audrey's would leave, then we'd be together. Audrey thinks I'm crazy about art, but it was really Luigi I was crazy about all the time. We kept getting crazier and crazier about each other. Then we decided to get married, and that's when things began to get really complicated. I just couldn't imagine telling Audrey. And Luigi's family wouldn't like it either, he said, with law school still to go to and everything. He minded being secret about it more than I did, but I told him I just couldn't face Audrey with it beforehand. I could just imagine Audrey going to his family to buy them off and how insulting she would be. Because they were nice people, Luigi's family, and they would be just thrown into a big mess by Audrey. You just don't know Audrey, or you'd understand all this. So finally we decided we would sort of compromise. We wouldn't run off to one of those funny places where you don't have to wait. We would just go ahead and get a licence and get married, right in New York, and that's what we did, all open and above board."

Dr. Finney said very gently, "Marie Louise, I'm asking you a lot of personal questions and you're being very sweet about it. I'll tell you something I didn't intend to. Nicole didn't have an 'accident' the way Hoopy told you. She was murdered—she died early this morning. And I'm not just curious about your personal life. I'm hoping that if I talk to enough people I'll pick up some thread that will help to show us why this happened to Nicole."

Marie Louise listened to this with the life and colour draining out of her face, and started to cry. "She was so sweet to us!" she said, choking on it, and Dr. Finney let her cry into her napkin for a couple of minutes before she said, "This all has to be done quickly, Marie Louise. Try to remember the happiness it gave Nicole to help you and Luigi, and stop crying and let me ask you some more questions."

Marie Louise sat there for a minute hiding her face, then she wiped her eyes and looked up uncertainly and said, "But I don't see what possible connection—"

"There may not be any connection. That's what I'm trying to find out."

"But it happened so long ago, two years ago, in America. I just don't see how it could possibly—"

"Do you know anyone who knows The Flea Club?"

"No. Except Hoop, of course."

"Does Audrey?"

"Know The Flea Club? Audrey? I don't know why she would," said Marie Louise, which told Dr. Finney what she wanted to know.

"What about a character named René Velerin-Pel?" she persisted.

"Oh, him! " said Marie Louise. "I know him all right. You mean the big handsome one. Audrey met him somewhere, I think we had an introduction to him or something when we first came over. He's an aristocrat or something. She made me go out with him a couple of times. She was always trying to get me to go out with men—like you, Hoop, but of course she always wanted to pick them out for me, the way she did you. I hated this René. He was supposed to be irresistible or something. And all the time, there I was, really married to Luigi."

"Did Audrey like René?"

"I think she sort of did. But I said I just wouldn't go out with him any more, I said I'd jump out the window first, so we haven't seen him any more."

"Indeed?" said Dr. Finney. "Well, let's not get off the track," she said, although it was obvious to me that she was going right down the track at full speed.

"You haven't told me the real reason why you wouldn't tell Audrey about Luigi, and I want to know. Trust me that there might be a connection."

Marie Louise was silent for a long few moments, and then said in a subdued and very serious voice, "Is there any chance I'd be getting Audrey in trouble?"

"There's not a chance that you'll get anybody in trouble except the person who killed Nicole."

Marie Louise laughed in real relief. "But that's perfectly silly!" she said. "Sometimes I think there isn't anything in the world Audrey wouldn't do to get her own way, but of course I don't mean she'd kill anybody." The last syllables trailed off a little bit as if, now that she had said it, she thought maybe Audrey could do even that, but then she brought herself up again and said with decision, "—and anyway, how could she possibly be connected with Nicole? So I'll tell you, but it's perfectly silly."

She spoke now with an effort at being casual, but there was plenty of strain involved, and still a lot more hurt than she was letting on. And by the time she had finished I knew why she had asked me, that first night, how much Audrey had paid me to tell her she was pretty, and why she had a profound lack of confidence in her own attraction, and why she thought (although she never said so) that she might not even be able to hold Luigi, although it was obvious to anyone who had seen them together that Luigi was hers for keeps.

"There was this other boy," she said, "two years ago. I met him on the train coming home from school; he knew one of the other girls. I was really young then, only sixteen, but I guess you can fall in love pretty hard at sixteen. Anyway, I did. He was a junior in college and we kept writing to each other. Then I visited this girl's family for a week-end and he came to see me, and he gave me his fraternity pin, and I honestly, I *honestly* don't think it was just—what Audrey said later. So we kept writing, but this school that Audrey had sent me to was terrible, and they told Audrey I was getting all these letters and specials and I had a fraternity pin. And that was awful, because I never wore it, except underneath my coat or something, and somebody must have tattled, or else they snooped at that school. Then Audrey acted as if she was being awfully sweet and everything and told me she wanted to meet the boy. And I don't know to this day what she said to him, but he began to be funny about things, and stand-offish. But what she said to me was that he was the most obvious kind of fortune-hunter and that I was crazy if I thought he would be interested in me when I was only sixteen and not very pretty or anything. Then I guess it was my fault, because I wrote him this long crazy letter about how he had to marry me right away or not at all, and, how I didn't have any money until I was nineteen, but if we loved each other we could get along. And do you know what happened? Nothing. Nothing at all. I never heard from him again, from then to this day. And I don't know what happened, unless it was really what Audrey said, fortune-hunting. But whatever it was, Audrey did it."

She stopped talking, compressing her lips tightly, whether out of anger, or to keep from crying, was hard to say. We all sat there a little embarrassed, until Mary Finney reached across the table and patted Marie Louise's hand where it lay on the table, clutching her napkin. Then Marie Louise said, "It used to hurt so much I would lie in bed and cry about it. So naturally when Luigi happened, I wasn't going to tell Audrey about it. I was just going to be horrid and wait until I was nineteen and had the money and then tell Audrey, because there's one thing you can do anything with Audrey with if you've got it, and it's money."

"You're not nineteen yet, and the cat's out of the bag," Dr. Finney reminded her.

"I don't care, though," Marie Louise answered. "I just don't care. I didn't know it then, but I know now that I can fight Audrey if I have to. And if Luigi wants my money, he won't have to wait long. Isn't that awful to say? But just because I can say it, I guess it means that I want him under just any circumstances."

I said, "Don't worry about Luigi. You've got him under any and all circumstances. Uncle Hoopy knows."

Dr. Finney said, "We can all take that for granted. You said you and Luigi were getting married, right in New York, all open and above board, except you weren't telling anybody."

"Yes," Marie Louise said, "but we had to tell just one little lie. We had it all arranged to get married on a Saturday morning, and when this friend of Audrey's in the Village called and asked me for the week-end, I said it was already arranged for me to stay with somebody else, and she said that was funny, because Audrey had explicitly asked her to jail me that week-end, although of course she didn't say jail, she said visit. But I said Audrey must have got her wires crossed because I was supposed to go somewhere else and I named the person. So Luigi and I got married Saturday morning and took a hotel room up-town, and I went back to classes Monday morning."

"You didn't even leave town? Suppose somebody had seen you in a compromising situation?"

"We thought of that. We decided not to worry about that, because if it happened it just meant that we weren't supposed to keep it a secret. It would be Fate. Anyway," she added, in perfect innocence, "we hardly went out of the hotel room."

I avoided any comment, but I caught Dr. Finney's eyes and she gave me a delighted glance in return. Marie Louise went on, "So we did the same thing the next week-end, and I told the same fib to this other friend of Audrey's, but then things really broke wide open because in the middle of the week Audrey showed up in New York and confronted me with those two week-ends. The first one she hadn't known about until she got wind of the second, and when she called that Village woman to check, and when she discovered I hadn't been there either, she nearly ripped things to pieces. She came to the school looking just as icy and calm as anything and she never raised her voice even once when she was talking to me. I suppose that's when I should have told her the truth, but I didn't. It was funny, but I didn't want to share Luigi with her, not even that much. I was scared of her too, but part of it was wanting Luigi all for my own secret. And so I just didn't tell her anything at all."

Dr. Finney said, "It isn't one of those freak wills, is it? There isn't anything in the will about your marrying or not marrying before nineteen, is there? Because I'm told those freak clauses don't hold water."

"No, nothing. It's just that I was so scared of Audrey. I'll be a little scared of her until I've got that money. I hate to put it like that, but that's the way it is. Money's the only thing that makes sense to Audrey—clothes and all that, it's all she really cares about. So all I could do was keep telling myself that I had to hang on because when Audrey was really dependent on me I'd have the whip hand. Doesn't that sound awful?"

"It sounds practical," Dr. Finney said. "I suppose Audrey yanked you out of school right away."

"She had me packed up and out of there in less than two hours. And when we got back home, it was terrible. Sometimes I would sit and look at the clock, just sit and stare at it, and think how many times the hands had to go around before five months would be up. I cried all the time."

"No wonder Audrey had psychiatrists in to observe you."

"She did not!"

"She told me she did. She said they came as guests."

"She had some awfully funny people around, but I didn't know they were psychiatrists. I bet they weren't very good ones."

"I'm sure they weren't. It is a noble profession, not given to sub-rosa investigations."

"Then we came over here. I still wouldn't tell Audrey anything, and she said there was only one reasonable explanation of what I had been doing those week-ends, that I must have been with a man or I'd be willing to say what it was all about. And she said to me, 'I'm taking you out of the country, Marie Louise, and if you've gone and got yourself pregnant, at least it won't show while we're at home, and whoever the man is,' she said, and then she said something I'll never forgive her for, never, not if I live to be a million years old; whoever he was, she said, and then she said *if* I knew his name at all, and that's what I'll never forgive, never—whoever he was, she said, I was to forget all about him and she was personally going to see that I met the kind of man who was an advantage for me to marry, and then she said we would just forget the whole unfortunate business, if I was lucky enough not to get pregnant, and we just wouldn't mention it again. She never once said anything that showed there was any possibility that if I had been with a man it was anything but vicious and nasty."

Marie Louise looked good and mad, and more grown up than I had ever seen her yet. "If she hadn't said that, I might have broken down and told her all about it. But then all this began. She whisked me over here and we had all these introductions and everything. I think I've been thrown at the head of every unmarried man in Europe who owns a set of evening clothes and has five dollars in the bank."

I said, "I'm flattered but puzzled to have been included. Audrey was doubtful whether I owned a tuxedo, and she didn't have any way of knowing whether I had five bucks in the bank or not."

Marie Louise said simply, "She was getting desperate. She was ready to try anything half-way presentable."

Dr. Finney let out one loud snort. I said to her coldly, "Did you want to add something?"

"No, no," she said. "You and Marie Louise are doing just fine. Go on."

"But then the worst part began," Marie Louise said, "because all this time I never did get to see Luigi. Audrey stood right over me in the dormitory while I packed my things to come home. I didn't get a chance until on the train the next morning, while Audrey was putting on her face. That takes all the work space there is in a compartment, so I told her I'd get out and wait for her in the diner. In the diner I wrote this note to Luigi and gave the steward a dollar to mail it. All I told Luigi was that we had to hang on somehow until my birthday and that Audrey was perfectly capable of reading my mail, so I said go out to the store at Sarah Lawrence and buy some notepaper with the school name on it like the girls use, and sign his name Mary but be careful not to really say anything."

For a minute there, Marie Louise had one of those split reactions where you couldn't tell whether she was about to laugh or cry. "Oh, his letters were so funny! I would know he was trying to say he loved me and missed me but they didn't make much sense, and once at breakfast I was reading one that had come special delivery and Audrey said who was it from, and what was so important that it had to come special delivery? So I said it wasn't important at all, and was from a friend of mine at school named Mary, who just sent it special delivery for no reason. I read it aloud to her, and all Audrey said was, "Well, your friend Mary sounds simple-minded to me, and you're too old for these schoolgirl crushes." But I left the letter lying open on my dressing-table because I knew she was going to poke around for it and read it to see whether I had really read it the way it was. It must have sounded perfectly pointless to her. And she never did catch on to anything at all.

"Then whenever I got a chance I would send these postcards from a drug store or something, to Luigi, and sign it Mario, and that's how I told him the name of the Paris hotel, I never thought he would follow me! And here I was all the time in the hotel, just crying and crying all the time, because I hadn't even had any letters signed Mary for two whole weeks, and poor darling Luigi was hanging around outside the hotel for days waiting for a chance to see me. Because when he called the hotel they would always ask who was calling, and anyway Audrey always took all the calls if she was in, and had the desk clerk take any messages and give them to her, instead of giving the calls to me if she was out."

I said, "I don't see quite what the advantage was to Audrey. She could keep you from getting married to somebody she hadn't picked out, but she couldn't keep you from getting to be nineteen, so what's the difference?"

"You'll have to ask Audrey about that," Marie Louise said. "What she does is beyond me half the time. She has her own way of figuring things out. The only thing she seems sure of is that the most complicated way is the best way."

"Go ahead," Dr. Finney said. "I'm dying for the part where you and Luigi get together."

"Well, I'd literally hardly put my nose out of the hotel for a week, and then only with Audrey, before that night when Hoop took me to the Opera. It's a wonder Luigi didn't die of pneumonia. He's awfully tough, though," she said with satisfaction. "Then when I finally came out of the hotel with. Hoop he followed us to the opera and followed us back, and then he followed Hoop to The Flea Club. And when you came out, he was waiting for you, and asked you about what kind of place it was. He didn't use that card you gave him, though. He followed you to where you live. But it was the next morning everything broke. You called me, and Mama told me I had to go out with you, and I said I wouldn't—that was when you heard me saying I wouldn't, I'm sorry—and she took the phone and began giving you all that goo-goo talk. I went over to the window and looked down into the street for no reason at all and what should I see but Luigi! There he was. I got out of that hotel so fast, I didn't even wait for the elevator. And when I said that I just went to a café and had a cup of chocolate, that was the truth, except that I had it with Luigi. And that sweet old thing had taken his law school money and followed me over, and he had told his family all about it and they had said for him to come get me, and he said all he wanted us to do was to go up to the hotel that minute and tell Audrey all about it."

"You should have."

"Maybe. But we had held out this long, and anyway now that he was here it was exciting, having it secret. We figured if you took me to The Flea Club and introduced me to Luigi there, maybe we could work it some way so Luigi could take me out, somehow."

"Audrey said you came back to the hotel after that cup of chocolate looking like death itself."

"That's what she told me too. She's always talking like that. I was so excited I had to hold myself in, and I had to go in and lie down before I could trust myself to talk to her at all. Then everything began working fine. Except that when we did meet at The Flea Club we knew we just couldn't wait. You know when Nicole met us and said was it our honeymoon? She was so nice."

"You really did know her singing?"

"And I really had her records. I didn't read about her in any paper, though. Luigi told me there was a singer named Nicole at The Flea Club you thought was good, and right away there was a reason to say I wanted to go there. And when you went down in the basement to look for Tony, Nicole said to Luigi and me that no matter what we said, she was a Frenchwoman and she knew better. She knew we had a secret of what she called a certain kind. And we told her the truth. It seemed perfectly easy and natural to tell her, because she had guessed it anyway just by looking at us, and she was so sweet about it, as if she was all happy for us even if she hadn't known us before. Then Luigi said this was the end. He said I wasn't going to go home that night, that I was his wife and I was going to stay with him, and I could go call Audrey if I wanted to. So I did. I was going to tell her. But she wasn't there.

"When I came back, Luigi was asking Nicole what would be a good hotel for us to go to, not too expensive, because his room was terrible, he said, and of course you can guess what Nicole said. She said we were to use her apartment upstairs, that she had a comfortable room downstairs she could sleep in. She said it would be a great joy to her to know we were there. That's what she said, 'a great joy'. And I think she meant it."

All of a sudden Marie Louise started to cry. "She was so sweet!" she said. "Nicole was the sweetest person! She was the sweetest person there is, except Luigi."

CHAPTER ELEVEN

THE WAITERS HAD dismantled and removed the ruins of the breakfast table, and Marie Louise was in the bathroom washing her face. The tears for Nicole had set her off into quite a little crying jag for things in general. After all, the kid had been under something you could call a strain for a long time.

I said to Dr. Finney, "Are we getting anywhere?"

"So far, so good. Hoopy, will you do a little leg work for me? Think you could get to Freddy Fayerweather and Tony Crew? Would they talk to me?"

"I could get Freddy here. He'll go anywhere and talk to anybody."

"Call him. The phone's in the hall."

Freddy's telephone rang five or six times, then a woman's voice said, "*Allô.*"

"Hell," I thought, "wrong number." I apologised and hung up, and gave the clerk downstairs Freddy's number again, asking him to get it right this time.

"*Allô.*"

Same woman.

I had a dizzy feeling of having to make a major readjustment. The voice was familiar now but not identifiable. Then Freddy's voice came on. "*Allô-allô-allô-allô,*" he carolled. "Hello hello hello and *good* morning. Who is it?"

"Me, for God's sake. Hoop Taliaferro. Where are you?"

"Home, dear boy! You called my number."

"Who's that woman and what's she doing there?"

Freddy said to somebody in French, "Come here, darling, it's Hoopy. Tell him hello."

"*Allô,* Hoo-pee," she said. "You teekleesh?"

Freddy said, "Thanks dear. Now give Daddy the phone. Hello, Hoop, wasn't that charming? Now. What can I do for you?"

"Is that really Bibi?"

"Of course. Who else?"

"What's she doing there?"

"Oh, dear boy, now you're *ask*ing. If you must know, she's living here."

"Oh, come on. What is this?"

"Life, dear fellow. Warm, beautiful, pulsating life. Life in La Bohème. All open, lovely, frank and unashamed. Bibi is now mine."

"Freddy, stop all this nonsense and listen to me. I'm at the Prince du Royaume and a friend of mine wants to talk to you. It's fairly important and I'm asking it as a favour. Can you come over?"

"*How* high can you *rise*!" said Freddy. "The Prince du Royaume, no less! Dear me! May I bring Bibi?"

"Yes. Ask for Dr. Finney's suite. Have you heard about what happened at the club yesterday morning?"

"About Nicole? Of course I've heard. Do you think I dwell in a world apart? How is she?"

"Don't be so flip. She didn't come out of it. Are you coming right now?"

"Just as soon as we can throw on our tiaras! Oh the things that have happened! You've—"

"*Missed* it. I know. Listen, where can I get hold of Tony?"

"What do you want of Tony?"

"I want to ask him a question. Come on, where do I find him?"

"Tony is the least of my concerns," said Freddy, too lightly, "but if you really want him, have you tried the police station?"

It was a good tag line and he hung up on it. Altogether, I felt as if somebody had pulled a rug out from under me and I had sat down hard. In this condition I came back into the living-room of the suite; Marie Louise was there, freshened up, which in her case was certainly an extra coat of gilt on the lily.

"Freddy'll be here," I told Dr. Finney, "and I think he'll be bringing a delightful surprise with him. But I can't get Tony for you because Freddy either doesn't want to give me his number, and I don't know his number, or else Freddy's serious about something I don't like. He says Tony's in jail."

"That's a help," said Dr. Finney, which I took to be sarcasm, until I saw she was serious. "I was just wondering how we could get Mrs. Jones over here, and this is it. Emmy, where's the little book?"

Emmy reached into an aperture in her garment and produced a small black address book which she handed to Dr. Finney. Dr. Finney flipped a few pages over, ran her finger down the line, and found a number. She handed the book back to Emmy and went to the telephone, motioning me to follow, and asked the clerk for the number. I could hear the thing ringing, then somebody answered.

"Hello," said Dr. Finney, giving her name and asking for a Monsieur Duplin. "Hello…Monsieur Duplin…Yes, fine, thanks…very comfortable, thanks. Nice place. Listen, Monsieur Duplin, what's this about Tony Crew being held?… Antoine Croute. He won't? Well what about the others?… Who, me? No, I haven't any ideas at all. What would I know about it? I don't know these people…Young friend of mine was concerned about Tony, young man you met the other morning just afterward, Mr. Taliaferro. I'll tell him Tony's all right. What I really called for, Monsieur Duplin, I want to get in touch with an American woman who's living here just now but I don't know how to reach her. Couldn't you look it up on a registration form or something? She's a conspicuous person and probably hard to get to—anyway, by one of my age and sex...Well, thanks, I'll be here whenever you call back." She gave him Mrs. Jones's name, and then said, in answer to some question of his, "No, I haven't forgotten, but I don't know what I'm going to say. You wouldn't just let me come to the dinner and not give any address?...Well, another thing. Would it throw your plans out of kilter if I brought a few interested guests along?...No, I mean in addition to Miss Collins... oh, maybe half a dozen...well, that's nice of you. Thanks. Good-bye."

Then she translated for me: "Tony's held because he won't say where he was from the time The Flea Club closed that night until he got back to his room late the next morning. The barman and all the other employees are accounted for except Bijou, and they can't locate her because nobody knows her last name or where she lives. He's going to call me back and tell me Mrs. Jones's address and number. He's still expecting me to make that goddamn address tonight and you're to come along as an extra guest—if you want to. How about it?"

"If I can stay awake. Who're the others, beside Emily?"

"How do I know, until I've talked to the rest of these people? Marie Louise, do you think your mother's up yet?"

"Are you planning to talk to Mama?"

"I am, or Hoop is."

"But what would Audrey know about Nicole? Or The Flea Club or anything that happened there? I don't understand all this. I see why you have a right to know why I was up there all night in Nicole's room with Luigi, and everything, but what do you want to talk to Audrey about?"

They were hard questions to answer tactfully and I didn't try. "Audrey's been seeing René at The Flea Club," I said, and the words hit Marie Louise with their total implication.

She said nothing, for a long quiet space, and I think she grew up another notch or two. Then she said, very low, "Oh, poor Mama. I'm so sorry."

The rest of us felt pretty damn awkward. Marie Louise stood up with sudden decision and said, "I'm going back upstairs and see her right now. I've been so mean to her, and told you all these things, and all this time she's been in her own kind of trouble."

"Does she know about you and Luigi yet?" Dr. Finney asked.

"Yes, she does. But I've been so terrible about it. When Hoop brought me back to the hotel that night I changed clothes and left a note for her. All I said was that I had been married for six months to an American boy and he had followed me here and I was with him, and for her not to worry about me because I was fine, but not to try to find me until I came home again, because she couldn't. I told her there was nothing she could do about any of it any more, and that I would call her the next morning. I signed it 'Love'. Thank goodness, I at least signed it 'Love'."

"Has she met Luigi yet?"

"No. She says she doesn't want to."

"When she meets him she'll feel all right about things," I said, crossing my fingers. "He's such a good kid. Do you want me to go up and tell Audrey how good I think the whole thing is? I had a long talk with her one afternoon—about you."

"I suspected as much. If you went up and talked to her now, would you be nice to her? Really nice? Kind?"

"I promise."

"She's so easy to be mean to. She acts so hard, and lays herself so open to it. I've been so awful."

"How is she now? Do you think she'd see me?"

"She's just sort of dead-acting. I don't know, why don't you call her?"

Audrey's voice on the telephone was as flat and listless as it had been forced and lilting when I had talked to her the other times.

"See me? What do you want to see me about?"

"About Marie Louise."

"She's not here."

"I know—she's here. I'm downstairs a couple of floors."

"Is that where she is? She said she was having breakfast with a friend. I took it for granted she was lying to me and was going out with this Luigi. Not that she doesn't have a perfect right."

"Let me come up."

She hesitated, and then said, "Oh, all right, come on. What difference does it make?"

She opened the door for me without any flourishes or suggestion, said, "Hello, Hoop, come in," noncommittally, and looked at me out of a face that had just plain given up. The make-up was bright, but perfunctory. Her hair was combed neatly, but it wasn't a big production job. She had on a pretty dress, since there was no such thing as an unpretty dress in her collection, but she wore it not for itself, but just because it was a dress and she had to be clothed. Don't ask me where the difference lies. Everybody knows it is there. There are ways of wearing clothes, and Audrey wore this dress with indifference.

When we sat down, she said, "I look awful," but she offered this as a piece of minor information, not the end of the world. "What do you want to tell me?"

"Marie Louise says you don't want to meet Luigi. I wish you would. You'd like him."

"I doubt it." Always that same listless tone. "I've been an awful fool. You did a marvellous job Monday night, didn't you? Practically helping them to elope."

"Look, Audrey, they've been married six months."

"Oh, I know. Nothing's your fault, of course. Everything's my fault. A grocer's boy."

"He's a damn nice kid. Also, intelligent and ambitious."

"Ambitious, obviously."

"He didn't even know Marie Louise had money. I mean he was ambitious to succeed on his own. He's going to study law."

"Oh, none of it really makes any difference," she said, with that same flat despair. "I've been such a fool, and I'm out of things. Out in the cold. Do you know what my allowance is, five weeks from now? One hundred dollars a week. My God, I'll end up in a boarding-house," and I saw that after all, she was still good old Audrey, thinking of herself first and only.

"What in the world makes you so sure of that? Marie Louise doesn't hate you."

"If she doesn't, she ought to."

"That may be true enough."

"You're very unkind."

"I don't mean to be. Tell me something, Audrey. First, though—please believe I'm here because I'd like to help. Will you believe that?"

"All right, if you say so. I haven't asked for any help. What do you want me to tell you?"

"What in the world would the advantage have been to you, if I had married Marie Louise?"

"That's not a question I'd call much help," she said, but she went on to tell me, anyway. She put her head on the back of the chair and closed her eyes. Every mark of middle age and fatigue showed clearly, yet it was a more attractive face than she had shown me yet. She went on speaking with her eyes closed, half as if to herself rather than to me. "You don't know what it is to be a person like me," she said. "I've always wanted so much, and when I married Marie Louise's father I thought I was going to have it. Then when he died I discovered I only had it on probation, and now I haven't got it at all. He wasn't anything of a man. I gave him all those years. It was just like him to die before his father and spoil everything. I've been so confused these last months. Up until then I thought it would still work out. I wanted Marie Louise to make a real marriage—truly, that was what I first wanted, something good for Marie Louise, a marriage with position and money. That's all that counts. I guess incidentally I wanted them for myself too. And I did everything I could to lead her in that direction. She says I was like a jailer and maybe I was. But that was what I wanted—the best for her."

She opened her eyes, and sat up wearily. "Well, how would you have felt in my place when you discovered—thought you had discovered anyhow—that Marie Louise had been sleeping around all over New York?"

"You should have known she never would. It's as simple as that."

"We won't argue it," she said. "As far as I was concerned, I had no reason to think she'd been doing anything but sleeping around. Then I took her out of school and this terrible time began. I told you I thought she must be psychotic, or whatever they call it. The way she moped around, wouldn't go out with men, all that. Well, I won't defend myself. I thought I had a piece of damaged merchandise on my hands and I also thought if I could find the right man to marry her…"

She stopped, and turned her head away.

"Me, for instance."

"This makes me sound so awful. Maybe I am awful."

"Get it off your chest. After all, it's practically in the family."

"All right. Marie Louise hated me, that was obvious. I'd done something or other to her she couldn't forgive—"

"You'd separated her from Luigi. Not to mention this other puppy-love affair you broke up."

"I wish she'd tell me half as much as she seems to tell you. I'd have understood."

"You don't understand now." I knew, because Marie Louise had told me, what she really couldn't forgive, and I had to remember that I was supposed to be kind to Audrey, in order to keep from repeating it.

Audrey went on, "She hated me, and here she was, almost nineteen. I saw I was just never going to get any of that money. And if she went out and married somebody, then they would both hate me, and it would be even worse—the way it's going to be now, with Luigi hating me too. But I thought if I found the husband—if he was somebody I picked out, somebody I could make a friend of, first—you, for instance—well, between you and me there might have been a kind of sympathy, an understanding, so that I wouldn't be thrown out—this is awfully hard, Hoop."

"You mean that if I married Marie Louise after the proposition you put to me, we could work it out so that after she was nineteen and the money was hers, you'd at least have the husband to get through to her with."

She lowered her eyes, pitifully ashamed, and said, "Yes."

"You and your daughter's husband would be accomplices against her."

"Don't put it that way. I can't stand much more of this."

"But, Audrey, it was such a poor plan anyway. Any man bastard enough to enter into an agreement like that would be bastard enough to leave you out in the cold. René for instance."

She jumped, and said, "Oh, God, you know everything."

"All I know is that you tried him on Marie Louise and it didn't take, and that I saw you at The Flea Club with him, and that you were described to me as his 'new one'. What I'm guessing is that when René smelt the money and Marie Louise was out of it, he turned his guns on you. I'm still trying to help, believe it or not. You know what René is, don't you? You can't not know. The kindest thing I can do for you right now is to tell you to drop René fast. He thinks the money is yours, doesn't he? Tell him it isn't, and you're out of trouble. Get rid of that one, and fast."

She was sitting up straight now, her hands clutching at one another, the fingers writhing and pulling like a nest of snakes. "I can't stand any more of this, Hoop. I can't stand it. I tell you I can't stand it. He's in my blood. My whole world's gone to pieces. I'm afraid I'll do something terrible. These last few days—that poor woman at The Flea Club—I need help! I need somebody—" and she went to pieces in the most horrible way, twisting her body back against the chair, in the worst fit of hysterics I had ever seen.

I ran to the phone and called Mary Finney. "Come right up here and come as a doctor," I said. "I don't know what you do for hysterics, but come do it for Audrey."

It couldn't have taken Mary Finney more than five minutes to get there, but I hope I never spend another five minutes as long as those. Marie Louise was right behind her, but I made her stay out in the corridor with me while Dr. Finney went in. I didn't want Marie Louise to see Audrey the way she was, although I couldn't keep her from hearing, which was bad enough. After a little while, the sounds quieted down, and Dr. Finney came to the door, still holding a hypodermic syringe. "Come on in," she said. "I had to sit on her to give her this stuff. Will you help me to get her to bed, Marie Louise?"

The two of them half carried Audrey into the bedroom, while she half protested, and I waited in the living-room. The telephone rang in the little hall; I answered it, and it was Emmy.

"Hoop, that Freddy person is down here. How is everything up there? Is Mary all right?"

"Yes, she won. Does she always sit on people to give them injections?"

"Frequently. It's a technique she developed to take care of people I'm unable to hold down. What shall I do with this Freddy person?"

"Engage him in conversation."

"We're beyond that already. I can't even get a word in edgewise."

"What's he talking about?"

"I can't quite figure out. He brought that girl with him."

"Bibi. How's she impress you?"

"Very quiet and sweet. But I don't think she's safe with that young man."

"Why not?"

"You know perfectly well what I mean. An innocent young girl alone in the city with a young blade like that. He's quite attractive and he looks unscrupulous to me."

"Well, he won't do anything irremediable to Bibi with you there. Hold it, and I'll be down."

I tapped at the bedroom door and told Dr. Finney that I was going down to her suite, because Freddy had arrived. "Wait a minute," she said. The door opened, giving me a glimpse of Audrey stretched out on the bed in her slip and stockinged feet, with Marie Louise standing beside her, bathing her face with a cloth. Dr. Finney came out, closed the door behind her, and said, "What in the world did you do to that woman?"

"I didn't do a damn thing. I was perfectly nice to her. She was perfectly all right until I mentioned René and told her if she was smart she'd drop him right away. Then she went off like that."

"Hm. Well, go down and take care of Freddy till I get there. Oh—Duplin called back and gave me Mrs. Jones's number. What's the best way to get her here, do you think? Using Tony's difficulties as bait, of course."

"How about getting your Monsieur Duplin in on it?"

"My idea was to put it up to her that through us she might help Tony without any contact with the police and hence the newspapers, etcetera."

"I could call her on that score, I guess. Freddy certainly could."

"Well, see if you can manage it one way or another. The number's in Emmy's little book now. I'll be down as soon as I'm sure it's all right to leave Audrey."

When I opened the door to Dr. Finney's suite, the sound of Freddy's yapping came rushing out as if the room had been filling with it like water piled up behind the door. He was standing in the middle of the room, carrying on, flanked by an audience of two women in chairs. Little Emmy Collins was listening with an expression in which amazement, incredulity and consternation were discernible. The girl in the other chair was not at first familiar to me.

"Hoop!" Freddy honked, stopping in the middle of a syllable and abandoning whatever he had been saying. "Dear fellow, good morning! I have simply fallen in love with your Miss Collins! If it weren't for Bibi, I'd *sim*ply ab*duct* her on the spot! Bibi dear, say hello to Hoop. Oh, dear, no English yet. *Bibi, dis bonjour à* Hoop."

"*Allô*, Hoo-pee."

"Not ticklish," I said. 'What in the name of Dior has happened to Bibi?"

"Marvellous, isn't it?" Freddy crowed. "Bibi, get up and show—oh, hell. *Lève-toi et*—how do you say it?—Bibi, get up and turn around for Hoop." He said it all in gestures too, and Bibi got up and obliged.

She was wearing a rakish black suit that Audrey wouldn't have been ashamed to be seen in, at a pinch, and she was lifted up to an elegant new height by the heels of her smart patent-leather pumps. Her legs, which had been all right, looked ravishing, and her black hat had been somebody's inspiration of the year. Beneath it her hair, the soft brilliant convincing yellow which a first expert bleach can achieve, was fashionably coiffed. Something had happened to her face. It was nothing but lipstick and powder and a little something for the eyebrows and lashes, but these were all just right for one another and just right for Bibi. Bibi had become a *poule de luxe*.

"Of course it isn't perfect yet," Freddy explained happily. "We have not yet begun to fight. The suit could be better. But what can you do, overnight? We have an appointment with Balenciaga next week. I think she's more Balenciaga material than Dior, don't you? And I'm teaching her to walk. Walk for Hoopie, darling. *Marchez, promenez,* get along with you. *That's* good."

Bibi stalked a few steps across the room and back, mannequin fashion, with fair skill. She came close to me, and smiled. The sweet meaningless little smile was still about ninety per cent the old Bibi, but it was changing, and she had learned a new phrase of English. "Is good," she announced complacently. "You like?"

"I crazy about," I said. "Is wonderful. *J'en suis fou. T'es merveilleuse.*"

"You buy me a drink?" suggested Bibi.

"No, no!" Freddy said. "No more drinks." Bibi pouted for us and then, smiling again, sat down and crossed her ankles nicely.

"Freddy, she's wonderful, but what I—"

"Pyg*ma*lion," Freddy interrupted. "I'm *ab*solutely Pygmalion. I got to thinking to myself, 'After all, Freddy,' I thought, 'you can't just go *on* and *on* doing—'"

"Wait a minute, Freddy, I'm trying to say that she's wonderful, but I want to know about Tony right away."

"But that's all part of it," Freddy said, "and I couldn't be less concerned. After all, I *tried* to protect Tony, and I was re*jec*ted, so if he needs my help now he can simply call for it, that's all." His voice was going shrill on him, but he brought it down again and said in a more controlled tone, "He can ask me for any help he wants and I'll give it to him the way I would to any good friend. Isn't that a reasonable attitude?"

"Seems to me you've been doing a job on yourself as well as on Bibi."

The quickness and naturalness and pleasantness of his smile were surprising. I had seen a lot of Freddy during the past several months and I had seen his face animated by all the exaggerations of expression which accompanied his affectations of speech, but I had never noticed until that moment that if I had ever seen him smile at all, it had been some kind of mocking grimace, or a simper.

"Indeed I have," he said. "I've begun a complete overhaul. But com*plete*, my dear."

"I," I said, "will be damned."

"Yes, I know," Freddy said. "*Too* fantastic. Of course it's going to take time. But I can't do everything at *once*, can I?"

"Don't strain yourself."

"You don't think I can do it, do you? I can, though. I just got to thinking, '*Look* at yourself, Freddy,' I said—by the way, I'm calling myself Gratzhaufer again—*look* at yourself, Freddy Gratzhaufer, just look at yourself ob*jec*tively, and what do you see? What's ahead?' I said to myself. 'Grab your bootstraps and pull hard, dear fellow, because why let things go on the way they're going until you end up on the confessional *di*van? I mean, why pay a psychiatrist for it when you can do it yourself?'"

"Freddy, I've got to sit down."

"Then let's."

We did.

Freddy went on, "Don't you want to hear about it? Do you want me to tell you? Of course I don't want to make a *nui*sance of myself, but I think being frank about everything is part of the cure, don't you? Does any of this bore you, Miss Collins?"

Emmy said, "I don't even know what you're talking about, but I'm fascinated."

"Well, that's very kind of you. Of course I'm not going to spend the rest of my life talking about myself. That's part of the change. I said to myself, 'Freddy,' I said, 'you *talk* about yourself too much, that's one thing.' But I think I ought to talk this *out,* don't you? I mean I think I really *should,* I think I *owe* it to myself."

"Then do."

"You saw it all beginning, anyway, in that awful scene down there in The Flea Club cellar, with Mrs. Jones. I hope you know I'd had a little too much to drink."

"That's not unusual," I said. "No crack intended."

"That's exactly one of the points, though," Freddy said. "That's one of the things I *looked* at in myself. So I'm having no more drinks. Absolutely none. But I certainly did have that night. And of course Hattie was *just* as drunk as an *owl.* Incidentally, I still think she's an *ab*solute *bitch.*"

"Steady on."

"Well, I do, and I won't be generous there. I mean, why hide it, if that's what I think? But when she said that about Tony saying I just bothered the life out of him—well, I knew it was true, even if I had never ad*mit*ted it to myself, and I suppose Tony really did say it to her. That was *aw*fully hard to take, of course, that he should say it to *her*, but I suppose it was *good*, really, in the last analysis, because it broke something. Hoop, I got *so* drunk, then. I simply bawled, with Hattie right there in front of me, just after you left

"That's why I left."

"—but I wasn't bawling over just that incident, I think I was bawling because there was already some kind of ter*ri*fic release and I knew this was some kind of *turn*ing point, or something. But I said awful things to Hattie. Really awful things, even considering who I was *saying* them to. Then she called me the worst thing of all, and tried to throw her highball at me, but she missed. Anyway she missed my face, it went all over my shirt front and in my lap. Then she left and I sat there dripping and saying to myself, 'Freddy, this is the low point of your life, the veritable *na*dir,' I told myself, and I saw what a perfectly silly ass I was. And I said I was going to change. But all I wanted right then was to be dead—not for keeps, you understand, but just for the night, so I could begin over again in the morning, so I began to drink as fast as I could. I just barely remember Nicole coming down there and seeing the condition I was in. I imagine Hattie sent her. Then she left and the barman came down and took me out the back door and put me in a taxi. I don't even remember Bibi coming down with the barman or getting into the taxi with me, but when it stopped in front of my place she was there, all right. My head was in her lap and I'd been sick all over the taxi floor."

Emmy looked at me in dismay, and Freddy said, "I'm sorry if I'm disgusting you, Miss Collins."

Emmy said bravely, "There are all varieties of spiritual experience and I'm sure some of the saints have had it in even more oblique forms than you did."

Freddy looked at her boggly-eyed, and so did I for that matter, and she said in a mousy little voice, "After all, it's the depth of inner experience that counts, not the associated surface manifestations. So I don't think Mr. Gratzhaufer's story is disgusting at all. That's what I'm trying to say."

"Miss Collins," Freddy said respectfully, "*where* do you come from?"

"She comes from Africa," I said, "where she packs nutshells."

"I'm a missionary, Mr. Gratzhaufer. A good missionary is a much more resilient person than most people suspect. We have to be. Please go on."

"I don't feel I have anything left to *say*, after what you said. When I woke up the next morning, though, there was Bibi lying alongside in all sweet innocence." (This required all Miss Collins's resilience, I knew, but Freddy carried on.) "She gave me a shower and made my breakfast and—there it was, that's all. The funny thing is, she seems to have had a yen for me all the time, and I didn't know it." He turned to Bibi and said, "*Dites à Madame si tu-m'aimes.*" Bibi said obediently with a sweet smile to Miss Collins, "*Oui, je l'aime,*" and turning to me she added slyly, "Is very teekleesh."

"See?" said Freddy. "So I thought to myself, 'Freddy, let's *create*. Begin anew,' I said to myself. '*Create*, dear fellow.' And so here we are. Of course it's only a beginning, but I think it's rather promising, don't you?"

"I'm not sure I like the hair."

"Neither am I. In fact I think the over-all effect's a little flashy. But Bibi wanted it that way. I've got to *lead* her. That's part of the job. I'll get things toned down eventually, but in the meanwhile I think it's really an awfully good start. Why don't you have lunch with us—all of you? Bibi simply must learn some table manners, among friends. What's holding your Dr. Finney?"

"I'll go see."

"And what was this important thing she wanted to see me about?"

Emmy said, "All she wanted to do was find out where you were at the time that—you know, Nicole. But you've already explained."

"Of course," Freddy admitted, "I could be *pay*ing Bibi to be my alibi, couldn't I? What I mean is, what's to prevent my having knocked Nicole in the head and then *pay*ing Bibi to say we were together all morning? But we were, actually. She was cleaning me up, you know, and then all that afternoon we were out trans*form*ing her. But really, she's too stupid to lie consistently, don't you think? I wouldn't take a chance like *that*. So I really think I have a very good alibi."

"Everyone seems to have the same kind of alibi, in this country," Emmy sighed. "I'm going to call Mary and see what's holding her."

She went out into the hall, and I took the opportunity to say to Freddy, "Are you really through with Tony? He might be in serious trouble, for all I know."

Freddy's lips jerked a couple of times before he was able to say, "I'd go through fire for him. I'm just trying not to, that's all."

CHAPTER TWELVE

EMMY CALLED ME to the telephone and I said to Dr. Finney, "What's holding you up there? Freddy's still here, and Bibi. Good has come out of evil again. They're transformed, reformed, and regenerated. As Freddy would say, you missed it."

"Well, hold them. I want to talk to them."

"They're already alibi-ed, if that's what you have in mind."

"The obvious one?"

"Yes. They were in the same place at the same time during the period in question. Freddy tries to imply that this is an understatement. Emmy, by the way, is getting quite Gallic. Took it all in her stride."

"I never worry about Emmy. Do you think Freddy could support his alibi?"

"I do. Freddy's concierge would probably remember what time they came in and what time they went out. It's an expensive place and they're careful about that. About opening the door, I mean."

"We'll let Monsieur Duplin make a routine check but I guess that's that. I've had quite a time up here."

"How's Audrey?"

"She's just gone to sleep. Ever hear of sodium pentathol?"

"It's an anaesthetic. I had it once for an operation. It was wonderful. Pure bliss."

"It's also one of the so-called truth serums, certain modifications of dosage and so on. Good relaxer and sedative, as it happens. That's what I gave Audrey. She began getting so truthful I had to send Marie Louise out of the room. In fact she's out of the hotel, that's why I'm stuck here with the sleeping beauty. Marie Louise is meeting Luigi and bringing him back for lunch."

"It looks like a jolly party. Freddy and Bibi want all of us, too. Don't leave me hanging like this. What was Audrey saying?"

"Come up here and I'll tell you. I don't want to risk it on the telephone. Maybe Freddy and Bibi won't mind entertaining Emmy until Marie Louise gets back. Did you get hold of Mrs. Jones?"

"Oh, Lord, I forgot. Freddy was so—"

"Well, do it now. Come up here and do it if you want to."

"Right up."

While Mrs. Jones's phone was ringing I said to Dr. Finney, "This isn't going to work, you know," and when it was answered, I got just what I expected. A secretary asked my name. I gave it to her, and could almost see her checking it against her book. Then, "I'm sorry, but this is an unlisted number. You must have dialled it by mistake. Will you please hang up and re-dial your number correctly?"

"It's not a mistake. I know I'm not on your list, but I have the number from a legitimate source. It's Hooper Taliaferro, and if she doesn't recognise that, tell her it's about Tony Crew and it's urgent."

"I'm sorry, but I am not allowed to accept your call."

"I'll hang up and re-dial this number in three minutes. That'll give you time to deliver the message, and if it doesn't work, you don't have to answer the telephone."

"I am sorry, I cannot deliver your message. Good-bye."

But when I called again in three minutes, Mrs. Jones answered the phone herself. "Oh, shut up, Harry," she said to somebody, and then, to me, "Who are you, anyway? I don't recognise your name. What is it about Tony? I hope I'm not going to have to have this number changed again. Do I know you?"

"In a way. We've met half a dozen times at The Flea Club. I was there in the cellar with you and Freddy Fayerweather for a few minutes two nights ago. Only you had my name wrong. You were calling me Harper."

"Oh, I think I remember. I'm sorry, Harvey. Well, what about Tony?"

"He's in jail."

"No! Tony? Whatever for?"

"Concerning Nicole."

"But that's absurd. Where are you? What can I do? *Oh, go away,*" she said to somebody, Harry, I supposed, "*let me alone, can't you see I'm—*"

A man's voice said, "I will take this call. Will you please tell me what your business is?"

"Certainly not."

"I am attorney for the party you have been speaking to."

"Get her to tell me that."

Mumble, mumble, mumble. Then Mrs. Jones, "It's all right, Harper—Harvey—"

"Hoop, but never mind."

"Go ahead and give this interfering jackass the message, since he wants it that way," said Mrs. Jones.

"It's short. Tony's in jail because he won't say where he was when Nicole was attacked. If you'll come to Dr. Finney's suite at the Prince du Royaume we'll talk about ways to get him out of trouble. If you're interested, that is."

She was interested. I had to say it all over again with elaborations and reassurances to the lawyer, but the end result was that they were starting immediately.

"She'll be here," I said to Dr. Finney, hanging up. "And she'll have her lawyer with her."

"Not a bad idea, either. That woman ought to carry a lawyer the way she does a handbag. Think we ought to let her and Freddy get into the same room, considering?"

"What's the advantage—or disadvantage? It might be spectacular. On the other hand, maybe they'd clam up."

"I dare say it would be the first time. We'll try it."

"About Audrey," I reminded her.

First, Dr. Finney called Emmy to ask if Freddy and Bibi were still there. Emmy reported that they were, but that Bibi was getting restless. She wanted to go out and spend a lot of money. Miss Finney asked Emmy to ask them if they could wait another half-hour, and got a yes. We went over and sat by a window, where we could keep an eye out for the arrival of Mrs. Jones at the entrance, and I gave a brief résumé of the Freddy-Bibi business, then I said please, I wanted to know about Audrey.

"There," said Dr. Finney, "is a really miserable woman."

The murder at The Flea Club brought me my share of confidences and confessions to listen to, but I will always feel that I was gypped out of the high point because I missed Audrey under sodium pentathol. But Dr. Finney said I wouldn't have liked it.

"I bet I would have," I insisted.

"No."

"Yes. I've always known she was a liar and I'd have been fascinated seeing what kind of truth those lies were germinated in."

"No," she repeated. "It was a kind of awful nakedness. It was sordid and pathetic."

Audrey, it appeared, had gone right on from where she had left off with me, except that, without restraint or inhibition of any kind, the story flowed from some dark, deep and terrible well into which Audrey herself had probably never dared to peer. It was all René, René, René.

"There's not a thing I can't tell you about that one," Dr. Finney said grimly. "The anatomical descriptions were explicit and detailed. That's when I sent Marie Louise out of the room. Master René's repertoire is beyond belief. A real stunt man. Nobody's got any objection to a little variety, of course. But what was so horrible, listening to that poor woman mumbling on and on about it, was that there was never the impression that on René's part there was ever anything but the most synthetic passion or desire, or even a good healthy interest in that kind of thing as a specialised sport. He's a technician, pure and simple—neither pure nor simple, of course, but you know what I mean. I'm a hard person to shock, when it comes to departures from conventional norms, and I like almost everybody. Most people's weaknesses are sort of endearing, once you come around to accepting them. But I don't accept René. What René does hasn't anything to do with weakness or pleasure or even personal viciousness. He's a sexual machine who uses himself to victimise women, and he certainly found a perfect subject in Audrey."

"A lot he's going to get out of it, with Audrey broke."

"I know. I'd like to be able to give out right now with a big horse laugh. Ordinarily I would—at both of them. It's always gratifying to see a vicious fool get caught in his own trap. Trouble is, I can't regard Audrey as a vicious fool any longer."

"Not vicious, or not a fool?"

"Neither, really. Just a scared desperate spoiled selfish woman whose only saving grace is a kind of innocence of the world, oddly enough. She's played the whole game at a very amateurish level, all the way through. And I imagine that she led pretty much a conventional and virtuous life while she was marking time married to Marie Louise's father, waiting for the money. Pretty much a conventional and virtuous and sterile life. You probably don't agree with me, but I suspect that René is her first extra-matrimonial adventure. And she's his victim, not he hers, don't make any mistake about that. These hysterics are nothing. She'll be lucky if she doesn't wind up with a good old-time nervous breakdown. As soon as René learns she hasn't got any of this money she's led him to believe she's got, he's off, and she knows it, and that's what's really driving her crazy. Believe me, Hoop, desire or passion or lust or whatever you want to call it—they give it funny names like hot pants, but believe me, it isn't funny at all, in a case like Audrey's, complicated by all her other confusions, especially. It's a torture. Audrey is really on the rocks."

"Odd thing," I said. "Even if Audrey really was as rich as she made a point of seeming, it's odd that René should drop Mrs. Jones for her. Jonesy's a lot richer and apparently was just as mad for him."

"What that's all about, I hope to discover pretty soon," said Dr. Finney. "Let's go down and give me a chance to see Freddy and Bibi before Mrs. Jones gets here."

"Can you leave Audrey?"

"For a few minutes. I'll send Emmy up."

The six of us sat in Dr. Finney's living-room—Mrs. Jones and Harry, Freddy and Bibi, and Dr. Finney and I. This lawyer, Harry, was about Mrs. Jones's age, which is to say, somewhere over forty or forty-five, and somewhere this side of complete dissolution. He was a smooth, soft-looking fellow who had had a good figure and now had that pushed-up-into-the-chest look that you get from an elastic abdominal band. He had once had a good Ivy League face, too. Vestiges of it still remained, especially in profile, but it had sagged badly without getting lined, so that it combined suggestions of both middle age and immaturity at once and unpleasantly. He was the kind of person who looks young for his age but about whose age there could never be any question. He was certainly attached to some firm with a top-ranking name, but if I had had to have any legal advice involving anything more complicated than, say, making a deposit with the gas company, I wouldn't have let him touch it with a ten-foot pole. I'm sure he was an honest lawyer, because the same set of social conventions which made it unthinkable for him to attend a formal dinner in his shirt sleeves also made it unthinkable that his firm should cheat a client, but if he'd had to choose between wearing the wrong dinner jacket and committing a felony, he'd have gone to pieces without arriving at a decision. He was well born, well bred, well connected, well groomed, and stupid.

"I want it understood immediately," he said, "that my client is here against my advice. I am present to protect her best interests and shall do so this morning, and in any subsequent circumstances resulting from this interview, with utmost vigour. I shall press to their most drastic conclusions any prosecutions within my power against any of you who take advantage of my client's presence here to force any issues contrary to her interests."

"That's just fine," Dr. Finney stuck in, as he paused for breath. "Hooray for you."

He went on talking, but I was watching Mrs. Jones. She seemed steadier and quieter than I had ever seen her. She sat there with an aplomb I had never associated with her before. As Harry droned on she sat politely waiting, quite at ease, and if she was feeling any agitation over Tony, or over anything, it did not show. Once she gave a sudden harsh, short cough, and reaching into her handbag she drew forth a small jewelled box and snapped the lid open to take out a small white tablet which she swallowed. She did all this in a precise, unhurried and steady fashion, whereas I had always thought of her as a person who made vague, jerky, haphazard movements. There was something very attractive about this new soberness of hers—and when the word occurred to me, I knew where the difference lay. She was sober. I had never seen Mrs. Jones before without a few sheets to the wind. She caught my eye as I stared at her, smiled as if at some small secret amusement, dropped the pillbox back into her bag, and turned her attention to what the lawyer was saying.

"...no connection whatever with the circumstances surrounding the accident suffered by the singer Nicole. In view of his close association with this woman and with The Flea Club, I have advised my client to avoid any communication whatsoever with the man Tony Crew, or Antoine Croute, now being held—"

"Harry," interrupted Mrs. Jones, "you are very dull."

"I am not trying to be entertaining."

Freddy let out a sudden cackle of laughter. Mrs. Jones said to Harry, "This is Freddy Fayerweather I was telling you about."

"But he was introduced to me as Grasshopper," said Harry. Freddy laughed again, but this time he had brought it down in tone, apparently not having liked the sound of his first outburst.

"Well, it's him, all the same," Mrs. Jones said.

"Freddy, who is this child? Is she deaf and dumb?"

"Don't you recognise Bibi? She doesn't understand English, that's all."

"I never saw her before in my life. You're sure she doesn't understand English? I've been wanting to say that she's terribly overdressed for her type. But she's a lovely-looking girl. Who's keeping her?"

"I am," said Freddy.

"Freddy! I couldn't be happier for you. Since when?"

"Since you threw that drink on me, two nights ago."

"What drink? Freddy, I never threw a drink on you in my life."

"Yes, you did. You said horrid things to me and called me a certain name and threw a full highball all over me."

"Freddy, that's absurd. It must have been somebody else. I wouldn't do a thing like that. Not to you. I'm very fond of you and I don't think you're a certain name at all. When other people say you are, I always deny it. Now, am I forgiven?"

"I've said I'd never forgive you. I promised myself."

"Well try, won't you?"

"What," I asked, "has all this got to do with Tony? The man Tony Crew, as Harry calls him, is languishing in the hoosegow. I thought everybody was going to get excited about it."

Freddy said, "I refuse to get excited about it. They won't hurt him. I'm not going to do anything about it."

"I'm not excited about it either," said Mrs. Jones. "Because I know exactly what I'm going to do about it."

"Hattie!"

"Oh, shut up, Harry. Dr. Finney, just exactly what is Tony being held for? Harry says one thing, but I never know when Harry's telling me the truth, and when he's doing what he calls looking out for my best interests. That always means keeping me from doing something I want to do. I think it's perfectly obvious from the life I've led in the last twenty years that what he thinks of as my best interests just isn't good enough."

"Hattie, that's not fair. At any rate, don't squabble in front of these people."

"Who's squabbling? I asked Dr. Finney a question, that's all, and you won't give her a chance to answer it."

I saw that poor old Harry was really put upon, no doubt about it, but I was unable to feel sorry for him.

Dr. Finney said, "Tony's being held because he refuses to say where he was during the time Nicole was attacked."

"Is that all? I knew Harry was lying. It's the simplest thing in the world. Tony was with me, as Harry knows."

"Hattie!"

"—and had been, all night. Ask the concierge. Ask anybody. Ask the newspapers, tomorrow. I just don't care. He saved my life, I really think. I told him I'd kill myself if he didn't take me home, and maybe I would have—although I doubt it, on second thought. Then I told him I'd kill myself if he didn't stay. So he stayed. What could be simpler?"

"Hattie," Harry groaned. "What good's a lawyer when you—"

"If you were any good to me yourself," Mrs. Jones began, "maybe I wouldn't have to go running around everywhere looking for—" which turned into the most tantalising remark made during the whole case, because it never got finished. The doorbell rang and she stopped right there. Everybody looked while I got up to answer it. It was Marie Louise and Luigi.

"It's the sweet pea!" carolled Freddy. They came in, and got caught in the business of being introduced around.

Freddy said, "I'm simply *lost.* I dis*tinctly* remember Hoop introducing you two to each other at my table, and now you claim to be husband and wife. *No*body can work *that* fast."

"It's too complicated to explain," Marie Louise said. "Hoop didn't know anything."

Freddy looked puzzled and said, "What did he intro*duce* you as? Not as a Mrs. Miss What?"

"It wasn't Miss anything," said Marie Louise. "He introduced me by my first name, like a little girl or something. It wasn't Miss anything. It would've been Miss Bellen."

Mrs. Jones and Freddy said at almost the same time, "*Bellen?*" and Freddy went on, completely out of control. "No! Don't *tell* me! It *can't* be! Don't tell me you're something to Mrs. *Bel*len!"

"Well naturally," Marie Louise said, "I'm something to *a* Mrs. Bellen."

"Mrs. Lemuel Bellen," said Mrs. Jones very carefully. "Audrey."

"Well, yes," said Marie Louise, perhaps apprehensively.

"Who is at this hotel," Mrs. Jones went on.

"Yes," said Marie Louise. "Do you know her?"

"In a way. Oh, yes, I think I may say that I know her, in a rather special way."

"Hattie. Please."

"Don't worry, Harry. If I could have found that woman several nights ago I wouldn't have answered for what happened. I could have killed her. But I feel perfectly calm about it now." It was true, she was calm. She was awfully calm. "I have a message for Mrs. Bellen. Some information, rather."

"Hattie, don't do this. I'm warning you."

"You're always warning me. You lied to me about Tony, didn't you? Did you lie to me about René?"

"Hattie, I won't be respon—"

"Harry, if you don't want a real scene, tell me now whether you lied to me about René."

"No I didn't. Not about the Gutzeit girl," and I saw Dr. Finney jump at the word. "That's the truth. You saw the photostats, for that matter."

"That's fine. Miss Bellen—I'm sorry, whatever your name is—do you think I could see your mother for five minutes, now?"

"I'm afraid not. She's sleeping."

"What I want to tell her," said Mrs. Jones, "will wake her up." Not long ago I had decided I liked her. Now I thought I had never seen anybody look meaner and more vindictive. I began to feel really sorry for Harry.

Dr. Finney said, "Mrs. Bellen can't be disturbed. She isn't well."

"That's a shame. I wanted to tell her this myself."

"*Hattie*, there's no point—"

"Shut up, Harry. Will one of you take a message, then? It's quite a message. I'm sorry to miss seeing her face. I'd like to see how somebody looks when they feel the way I felt. I wanted to marry René, you know."

Harry had stopped saying "*Hattie!*" by now. He would moan softly from time to time, that was all.

"Mind you," said Mrs. Jones, "I don't mind her having him. Not at all. It's a matter of complete indifference to me. She's welcome to him. I did mind her making a play for him while I had him, though. At the time, I was wild. Funny thing is, I thought she had won. I suppose all of you saw me getting ditched."

"Oh, yes," said Freddy. "*I* did."

"I know you did. You were enthralled. You loved every bit of it. This fool here," she said, nodding towards Harry, "was protecting me again. I admit he had a point. René's really a leech, and I'm well out of it. Do you want to tell them what you did, Harry?"

Harry's face looked like the inside of a large sweaty hand. He managed to say, "Our firm, representing our client's best int—"

"No!" commanded Mrs. Jones.

Harry said miserably, "This is extremely distasteful. Concerned over the, um, acquaintance of our client and this man, we sought to discourage her interest, but failing, we set a rather large force of detectives to doing research into his past. We found that he is already married."

"Pooh," said Dr. Finney smugly. "*I* knew that." I said nothing because I was incapable of it.

Mrs. Jones said, "You knew it? Did you know this woman? This what's-her-name?"

"Not exactly," said Dr. Finney.

"Gretel Gutzeit," said Harry.

Dr. Finney said, "What?"

"Her name was Gretel Gutzeit," Harry repeated.

"Dear me," said Freddy, "how un-René-sounding!"

"You should have seen her," said Mrs. Jones. "I saw her picture. She could hardly have been less René-looking. Side of a mud fence."

Something very curious was happening to Dr. Finney's face. It began to glow as if with an inner light, but not with a light which was generally diffused. It was a very spotty inner light, of an orange colour, and it appeared to be increasing in intensity so that the speckling of small holes through which it shone grew more and more orange. I saw, then, that Dr. Finney was not glowing with an inner light at all. She was growing very pale, and her orange freckles were standing out against the oystery background of her face instead of blending into its usual ruddy pink.

"...could have told me," Mrs. Jones was saying, "but like a fool," which by now I knew was Harry's appellation, "he chose to tell only René. Oh, that was bright! He told René what he had found out, but that he would not let it go any further if René dropped his pursuit of me. Poor me! And all the time

I had been begging him to marry me, and wondering why he wouldn't. Everybody else did. Oh, dear, he had such curious explanations, all mixed up with honour. For delay. Then when he suddenly shifted to this Audrey bitch—I do beg your pardon, Mrs. Beld—Bald—whatever your name is, child—I made this utter spectacle of myself, coming around The Flea Club and screaming, and ready to tear this Audrey bitch apart if I found her. All of you saw me, I suppose, anyway most of you, and I hope you understand now. It wasn't my fault at all, it was Harry's and I didn't get jilted at all. Not at all. But I thought I had been, and that's how Tony happened. You know, I can't even remember falling in love with Tony. But I am famous," she said, "for my rebound."

Harry raised his hands and let them fall, in a gesture of utter resignation and despair.

"And so now I think I will go," said Mrs. Jones, grasping her handbag and rising from her chair. "Harry."

Harry rose also, with all the spirit and vigour of an old whipped dog. Mrs. Jones said, "So—if some of you will relay my message to Audrey. You've all been very sweet, and I've loved seeing you. We must all get together again soon. Don't worry about Tony. I'm going now to bail him out." Her eyes moved over us, one at a time—Bibi, Freddy, myself, Dr. Finney, Marie Louise, and then stopped on Luigi.

"Have you been here all the time?" she said. She looked him up and down and said, as if for future reference. "You're terribly handsome. Well—good-bye for now, everybody," and out she walked, with Harry following on his leash.

CHAPTER THIRTEEN

THE MINUTE THE door closed behind Harry and Mrs. Jones, Dr. Finney jumped up and said, "Freddy, thanks, but we can't go out to lunch. Now you and Bibi go away. Oh, I forgot—if you want Bibi to learn manners, I've got just the place. We want the two of you to come to dinner with us tonight. There'll be some other people there—maybe about a hundred—but we're having a special table. It's a kind of celebration for me and I'm giving a talk. Emmy'll call you about the place and time and all. Good-bye now," she said, not even waiting for Freddy to say he would or wouldn't come.

She continued to fidget while Freddy explained to Bibi the proper way to make her good-byes, which she did very prettily, and they left. Then Marie Louise said she was going right up to stay with Audrey, and would order lunches for herself and Luigi in the room. She kissed Dr. Finney on the cheek, startling her a little, and then turned to leave with Luigi, saying she would send Emmy down. "No," Dr. Finney said, "order a lunch for Emmy too. Hoopy and I have errands to do and Emmy'd love company. Hates to eat alone." So that was arranged, and Marie Louise and Luigi left, and Dr. Finney and I were alone in the apartment.

She had a tense, brisk, no-time-for-questions look about her that kept me quiet while she charged over to the telephone and, after a respectably brief interval, got Monsieur Duplin on the line. It was Dr. Finney, she explained, and Mrs. Jones was on her way to bail Tony out, with a lawyer, and as far as she was concerned, Dr. Finney that is, it was O.K. for Tony to be bailed out or whatever the French equivalent was, if Monsieur Duplin wanted to release him, and although she would have preferred to talk with Tony herself, if possible, she was sending a Mr. Taliaferro down instead, which told me what my errand was. And, if possible, please delay things with Mrs. Jones until Mr. Taliaferro was also on hand. Possible?

She said thanks, hung up, told me to put on my coat and hat, said I was going to go in a taxi with her as far as The Flea Club, where I was to give her my key and drop her, and then I was to go on to witness whatever spectacle took place, if any, between Tony and Mrs. Jones and Harry, and report everything to her in detail.

"I don't suppose you've thought about Taliaferro's lunch?" I asked, when we had got under way in the taxi.

"You can eat later," she said. "I don't want you to miss Jonesy."

"And what will you be doing all this time?"

"I'll be wandering around The Flea Club."

"Just why?"

"Just to see whether anything suggests itself. There are loose ends. Old Bijou is the loosest. She's a faithful-retainer type, isn't she?"

"The most faithful and devoted imaginable."

"Yet she seems to have lit out. With the missing cash box, if you want to make things simple, but it seems too simple."

"Not consistent with Bijou, either. Very poor but, as far as Nicole was concerned, very honest."

"Missing, nevertheless, which must be explained," Dr. Finney said. "And I've simply got to get to René. Preferably before the dinner tonight, but try to get in touch with him and if I can't see him before the dinner, be sure he comes to that, anyway. One hell of a lot revolves about him. And when you see Mrs. Jones and Harry, make sure you ask them for tonight."

"It's a charming guest list you're working up. Half the people on it ready to cut the throats of the other half, and more bed and re-bed combinations than you could shake a copy of Krafft-Ebing at. A divine little crew. Also you've a naïve faith in my ability to coerce these people into dining with the police. Do you know that Mrs. Jones is an international socialite? You don't get her to dinner on the spur of the moment."

"The spur of this moment," Dr. Finney said, "is like the spur of no moment she has ever experienced. Who's this famous party-arranger? Elsa Maxton or something? Maxwell. Elsa Maxwell'd give ten years of her life to fix a party with half the novelty mine's going to have. You ask these people. They'll come. If not from curiosity, then through fear. Supposing you'd knocked Nicole on the head. Wouldn't you be afraid not to attend something where you might be so suspiciously conspicuous by your absence?"

"I might, if I were bright enough. I'll try, anyhow. Try to get everybody for you, I mean."

"Good boy. Now pass me that key." She told the driver to stop at the Deux Magots, an unsuspicious spot, so she could walk to The Flea Club from there. She got out of the taxi and strode down the boulevard without a backward glance and, as I watched the firmness and decision of her gait, I was awfully damn glad I wasn't hiding anything in particular that she was interested in ferreting out.

At the *mairie* where Tony was being held, I was directed with a degree of respect that indicated the eminence of my connection with Monsieur Duplin and Dr. Finney to a small close waiting-room smelling of damp wood and disinfectant, where Mrs. Jones and Harry occupied one bench, and an extremely discouraged-looking girl of about twenty occupied the one opposite. With a Freddy to put her into the hands of the technicians who had overhauled Bibi, she could have been ravishing, but she looked cheap, dishevelled, and badly worn as she sat there in the evil little room. As I entered she shifted her glance from Mrs. Jones to me, sized me up as another member of the class in league against her, and began staring at an empty corner of the room in resentful pretence of indifference to the three of us.

When Tony appeared in the doorway she was on him in a flash, clawing at his shoulder as if she would tear him apart, and for a moment I thought she was attacking him, until I saw that it was a kind of frenzied embrace. She babbled to him in French so disfigured by argot and so muffled by the crazy rubbing of her face against his shoulder that I could catch only phrases: "... darling...do to you?...hurt you...take you from me...darling..." Tony looked much less immaculate than usual. His shirt was tired and he hadn't shaved; his beard made a pattern as sharp and even as a stencilled one around his lips and up his cheeks. He was pale, and in this sordid little room his jacket with its padded shoulders and tight waist, wrinkled now around the buttons, looked sleazy and raffish. His expression was at once tense and closed; it did not change as he found the girl's wrists and, gripping them, forced her away from him. He spoke to her in a voice too low and guttural for me to catch anything he said. She wailed, and struggled to press herself against him once more, but the officer who had followed Tony into the room took her firmly by the elbows, and as Tony released her, this man propelled her back to the bench and forced her down on to it. She sat there, obedient to authority as she had learned to be as long as she was in its presence, glaring at the officer in hatred and despair.

Mrs. Jones had watched this performance with the air of royalty in the presence of vermin. She rose now (while Harry jumped to attention, making uncertain twitching motions which indicated that he was looking out for her best interests) and said, "Tony, who is this girl?" The officer told her she would have to speak French. She repeated the question, translating it literally, word for word, so that "girl" took on its unflattering connotation. "*Salope!*" the girl shrieked. "*Chamelle!*" Tony said nothing, but I looked at him and thought that this boy who now looked like a common boulevard pickpocket or café procurer was the same boy who, neat and enigmatic at The Flea Club, had seemed impervious to its excitements, vanities, and frustrations. As he stood there, unspeaking, in the few seconds we waited for him to answer Mrs. Jones's question, I realised that I really knew nothing about Tony. He had a neat, taut figure; he had attractive, symmetrical, well-washed features; he had a genuine facility as a kind of glorified street musician; above all he had the ability to keep his mouth shut and his face blank. But what he was really like, I simply did not know, because he hid it. And it occurred to me for the first time that perhaps Tony really was a son-of-a-bitch, and that at least one of the inconsistencies Mary Finney was always looking for and then trying to explain, was that Mrs. Jones had fallen for an un-son-of-a-bitch when her eye up to then had been infallible in picking out the real cream of that crop, and that even if she didn't know Tony was a son-of-a-bitch she had developed such a sensitivity to the type that perhaps Tony wasn't an exception, but the logical successor to her Italian count, her Georgian prince, her English jockey, her American prize fighter, and René. I had an odd and uncomfortable feeling, partly because I was aware of a disloyalty to Tony because my mind was changing about him when he was in a tough spot, and partly because I felt a sense of loss that a person I had thought was just naturally good was, maybe, not good at all. I realised that Tony had carried quite a burden for me, representing, all alone, man's innate capacity for goodness in spite of the general brutalisation, deception, and chicane of the world. Now I thought he had dropped the ball, and whether or not the curious guilt I felt meant that I had failed somewhere, I knew I'd never feel the same about Tony again. I wouldn't have put it all like this at the moment; all I knew was that things changed, and left an uncomfortable empty feeling behind them.

CHAPTER FOURTEEN

THE VARIOUS THINGS that happened during the next three quarters of an hour in that room were so broken up and confused that when I tried to summarise them for Mary Finney afterwards, I couldn't put them into anything like their original sequence. Boiled down to essentials and put into some kind of order, things went like this:

Mrs. Jones demanded again to know who the girl was. Tony finally answered, in a sullen and defeated way, to the general effect that she was simply his girl, that's all. Mrs. Jones took this so hard that she didn't even scream; she just grew rigid. She should have been accustomed to sharing her men, none of her claims having been the original ones and all of them having proved to be temporary in any case, but she was accustomed to the marital rotation conventional within her own international circle, whose membership was elastic enough to encompass attractive males from the race track, the prize ring, the lower reaches of Bohemia, or the metropolitan jungle which had produced Tony, but could not stretch wide enough to include the females originally appended to these candidates. Tony's misfortune was that he was caught between his past and his future at the awkward moment when he was engaged in the transition from one level to another, and it was obvious that Mrs. Jones felt sullied. She felt so sullied that she sat down on the bench and got out the little box again from her handbag and took a pill. "Harry!" she commanded. Harry plopped obediently on to the bench beside her. She began to whisper to him, and if I could have heard at all, I was prevented from it by the arrival of Freddy Fayerweather.

I should have been ready for this. In spite of all his good intentions for reform, and in spite of his contention that he would be willing to strangle orphans, Freddy was too kind-hearted and too weak-willed to stay away from Tony when Tony was in trouble. He entered accompanied by a pleasantly potbellied and keen-eyed little Frenchman whom I identified as Dr. Finney's Monsieur Duplin even before he introduced himself.

Freddy cast Tony a quick, uncertain glance, looked at me in surprise, and then said to Mrs. Jones, "But Hattie *dear*! I didn't think you really would!"

Monsieur Duplin explained then that Freddy had come to him with the statement that if Tony refused to say where he had been at the time of the murder, he, Freddy, had heard a verbal statement from a lady that Tony had been with her at the time. He had come to Monsieur Duplin to ask him to face Tony with this information, and to get Tony to identify the lady. "Although of *course* I'd have done it myself, if Tony refused," Freddy admitted, "and of course I wouldn't have bothered if I'd known you'd really be down here, Hattie. I must say I think it's big of you. Sacrificing your repu*ta*tion," he said, managing to infect the word with a strong suggestion that the remaining shreds and tatters of Mrs. Jones's good name were hardly worth the effort, "for a simple boy of the streets. Really too *sweet* of—"

But Harry rose, interrupting, "My client denies the allegation."

Tony jumped as if from a blow. The girl sprang up so suddenly that she was half across the room before the officer caught her. "It's true!" she shrieked in an ugly voice. "*Salope! Chamelle!* So that's where he was! Not even a woman! A skeleton! He didn't come home, not at all." And even in French it wouldn't be right to put down what she began calling Mrs. Jones, but it boiled down to a general reference to ugly old cadavers who bought young men with their dirty money. The girl had real skill in invective, and it would have been a devastating experience even for a woman less vulnerable to the accusations than Mrs. Jones. The officer stopped it with a hand over the girl's mouth.

Monsieur Duplin asked Tony if he wanted to say anything now. He looked uncertain and shifty, obviously balancing several desperate factors against one another. Finally, deciding, he began, "I—" but his voice cracked so that he had to clear his throat and begin again. "Yes, I was with her," he said.

"My client denies—" piped Harry, but Mrs. Jones rose and stopped him. The room grew quiet as everybody waited for her to speak. She said with admirable aplomb, considering what she had been going through, "Very well. That is true. He was with me." Tony looked like a man caught up off the brink of a precipice. "However," said Mrs. Jones, looking at him with distaste, "he was not with me after six o'clock that morning. I didn't know you were a fool, Tony. We could have got you out of this some way, but you've been a fool. I'm not going to compromise myself." She laughed a little bit at the word, and corrected herself, "—with the law, I mean. Nobody wins now." She said to Monsieur Duplin, "This boy was with me that night but he left my house at six in the morning. I'm sure that can be verified by the night servants if you're interested. I've no idea where he went after that. Nor do I care. Come, Harry." She swept to the door, turned, and looked at Tony but said to the room in general, "This was the quickest one I ever had." She paused a moment, and added with considerable satisfaction, "And by far the least expensive." Harry groaned, and followed her out the door.

Now it was Tony who was shattered. I have thought and wondered about Tony a lot since these events. In retrospect I think it is possible to believe that he was, once, what he had seemed to all of us—a really good and honest kid, but not as strong a one as he seemed. The thing about Tony and The Flea Club is that he wasn't attracted to it by temperament; he was there to make a living, and once there, he was debauched by it. With a background like Tony's you can't see so much conspicuous sonofabitchery among the moneyed without wondering why a little more of the money shouldn't come your way, and I dare say that Freddy aggravated this dissatisfaction by needling Tony with the idea that his importance to Nicole and The Flea Club was greater than he was getting recognition for on his pay cheque. For that matter this might have been true, because Nicole was at heart a shopkeeper who was keeping expenses down. If it was true, it would have been the strongest kind of goad to push Tony into a profitable liaison with Mrs. Jones. But the timing had been terrible, and Tony stood there in front of us not only without honour, but without any compensation, either material or spiritual, for its loss. And from this desolation he began answering Monsieur Duplin's questions.

Yes, it was true, he said, that he had left Mrs. Jones early that morning. They had gone all the way to her place outside Neuilly in a taxi that night before; he had paid for it, and it had left him without enough in his pockets for breakfast. He had had to walk to the Metro, which had taken close to half an hour, then he had gone to The Flea Club, to ask Nicole for an advance, if she was up, and to fix himself some breakfast in any case. He let himself in by the cellar entrance, with his key. Bijou was already there, but hadn't begun to straighten the place up. She was sitting at one of the tables with a pot of coffee and a loaf of bread and some butter. He had sat there sharing the breakfast. They were surprised when Nicole came in from the cellar bedroom. She was wearing a dressing-gown. She had spent the night there because she was too tired to climb the stairs to her own room, she had told them. Tony asked her if he could have some money; she had gone to fetch the cash box and had given him an advance without question. She had had a cup of coffee and a piece of bread. She reminded him that they were to rehearse that morning, but had asked him not to stay around, but to come back later, around 10:30. This had struck him as odd, and he had no explanation for it. (I had: Marie Louise and Luigi.) When he left, Bijou was cleaning up the breakfast clutter. If they wanted verification of all this, he said, they could ask Bijou. He said this so naturally—at least as naturally as he was able to say anything, in his state—that I could see no reason to believe he knew that this was the last thing, so far, we knew about Bijou.

Since Nicole had asked him not to hang around the club, he was left with an awkward interval of time to kill, and being a good Frenchman, he decided to kill it in a café. With money fresh in his pocket and, he thought, a rich woman who would keep him supplied with more from now on, he went to the Deux Magots instead of one of the smaller inexpensive places he would ordinarily have used, and had a cup of coffee. Perhaps the waiter could verify this. But he had felt restless, and had left the café.

He hesitated then, and when Monsieur Duplin told him to go ahead, Tony said, "You are not going to believe me."

"That is not your affair," said Monsieur Duplin. "Tell me the truth."

"I went to a church."

"Very well. What church?"

"To St. Sulpice."

"What did you do there?"

"Nothing. I took a place in the back of the church."

"Very well. How long did you stay?"

"Perhaps half an hour."

"And then?"

"There is a gramophone shop at the corner of the Boulevard Raspail. I went there."

"Can you verify that?"

"No. I did not go into the shop."

"Then why did you go there? Tell your story without these questions."

"I went there because there was a display of Nicole's records. It gave me pleasure to look at them with my name on them. I have done this before. Then I walked along the boulevard looking in other shop windows. Then it was time to appear for rehearsal so I walked back to the club. But I did not go in. There was a police ambulance in the street. They put Nicole in—I did not know it was Nicole, but who else could it be except Nicole or Bijou?—and then a policeman remained at the door. I did not want anything to do with the police. So I went home. I stayed there until you came for me. That is all."

Monsieur Duplin stood contemplating Tony in silence, as we all stood waiting for what he was going to say. When he spoke, finally, he said to the officer, "This man is to be discharged." The girl gave a wailing cry of relief. Monsieur Duplin looked at her and added, "—but this woman is to be held." The girl was stunned into silence.

"Take the woman," Monsieur Duplin said to the officer. "The man will come with me."

All this time, Mary Finney was at The Flea Club. She went with no definite idea in mind, she told me—that is, with no definite question she thought she might find the answer to. She wanted to see whether the place itself might suggest questions and answers, not necessarily by anything new she would discover there, not necessarily by anything tangible, but by the general air and suggestion, through a kind of osmosis. She wanted to try to visualise some of the things I had told her, she said, in the places where they had happened.

She let herself in by the cellar entrance, closed the door behind her, and stood for a few moments looking at the dim, suggestive room. The greyed winter light seeped down from the small high windows leaving the corners in obscurity. The place was as cold, she thought, as a tomb, and the word *tomb* kept playing in her mind. Professor Johnson's two great pits, empty and desolate, sank into the floor as if they were bottomless. She walked now between the crowded tables and stared into these pits, thinking how like they were to graves waiting for bodies. Then, turning from them, she tried to visualise the room full of the night crowd, with Nicole singing and Tony playing. She tried to visualise Tony and Freddy and Mrs. Jones as I had found them there that evening, Freddy and Mrs. Jones arguing over Tony as if he were up for sale (as indeed, it now appeared, he had been) and, finally, Tony leaving and Mrs. Jones wailing that she loved him. Then she tried to see Mrs. Jones and Freddy, as Mrs. Jones threw her drink over him, and then Freddy alone, as he sat there in humiliation and degradation. She tried to imagine Bibi finding Freddy, and taking him out to a taxi. She went over to the small bedroom, imagining Nicole there, and imagining her getting up, that morning, to admit somebody who had sat with her at a table, with a glass of whisky and soda, and then killed her. She didn't know, yet, what I was learning at that time—that Bijou had arrived, according to Tony's story, and then that Tony had let himself in, finding Bijou there and sharing a breakfast with her, before Nicole appeared and fetched the cash box to give him an advance.

Dr. Finney went upstairs to the bar, then, and tried to imagine it smoky and crowded, with Bibi at her station waiting for "teekleesh" customers. She imagined Luigi there, stringing me along and then meeting Marie Louise. She imagined Audrey with René, Tony with Freddy, Nicole singing, in her glamour make-up and her lamé gown, instead of soiled, crumpled, and bloody as she had seen her that morning. Going upstairs she imagined Mrs. Jones in hysterics as Tony held her and Nicole slapped her face to bring her round. She went into Nicole's bedroom and imagined Marie Louise and Luigi there, imagined me banging on the door, imagined them scurrying downstairs and out the boulevard door while I more or less stood guard for them.

Here Dr. Finney made a brief telephone call to Emily Collins. Then she went downstairs to the cellar again and recalled in detail the only part of the whole story, up to that point, that she had been directly a part of. She re-enacted our entrance—Emmy's, Professor Johnson's, mine, and her own, and our discovery of Nicole. She sat at the table where Nicole had sat, sat there for a long time in the near-dark, thinking that she knew what had happened to Nicole now. Then the telephone rang.

As soon as I got away from Freddy and Monsieur Duplin, I went to a pay station and rang The Flea Club. Dr. Finney answered, and I gave her the gist of what had happened that afternoon. She asked me a couple of questions, particularly about Tony's account of his morning, and I answered them, in line with the summary I have just given of what had been going on. Then she asked me how many of the guests I had lined up for that night. I hadn't done very well, but told her I would get on the ball and do everything I could. She told me she would see me at the hotel half an hour or so before dinner—she didn't think she'd have time to change—and then she hung up.

Then she crossed directly over to the corner of the room where Professor Johnson's workmen's tools were stacked, selected a shovel, turned on the lights, and began to dig. After five minutes or so she had discovered what she expected to discover. Then she sat down again and did a final job of putting her information, her theories, and her surmises into order.

She never said so to me, but I know damn well how she felt: she felt smug.

CHAPTER FIFTEEN

THE BLUE WINTER twilight had already set in when I got back to the Prince du Royaume. Emmy let me into the suite. She was, in a way, all dressed up, which meant that she had changed from one indescribable garment to another, and had a general look of being freshly talcumed.

"I thought I'd get ready for the party early," she said. "Things have been so quiet around here."

"Where I was they weren't," I told her. "Also I'm behind in party arrangements. I've got to get hold of the rest of these people and see that they get there."

"I've taken care of some of that," Emmy said. "Things have been quiet but I didn't mean nothing's happened. Quite a bit has happened. I've several things to tell you, and I'll begin immediately." She had a list of reminders, written on a small neat card, which she checked herself against from time to time.

"In the first place, I'll tell you about Audrey," she said, "partly because it sounded so important at the time but turns out to mean nothing at all. Marie Louise called down and said Audrey was awake and terribly worried about something she wanted to tell Dr. Finney. I said Mary wasn't in but I would come up if that would help. Audrey didn't like that very much but I told Marie Louise to tell her that I'd relay whatever it was to Mary just as soon as I saw her, which would be before Audrey could see her, so Audrey said for me to come on up. Gracious, she did look pitiful."

"She's been having a rough time."

"I know. At first I thought she might be worried about something she had said under the sodium pentathol, because Mary says she did do quite a lot of talking about extraordinary things. But they don't remember what they say, you know."

"She's lucky, then."

"But it wasn't about anything she had already said. Do you know, she called me up there to tell me a perfectly pointless lie."

"That's the way she is. Sort of feels that almost any lie is a kind of protection, just by virtue of not being the truth."

"Isn't that pitiful? Well, she beat about the bush in the most elaborate manner, but what it came down to was that she wanted to tell me she had been with René that morning when Nicole was attacked. They were not in either of their hotels, she said, and of course that's the kind of thing the police can check."

"They might have been somewhere else for the night."

"I don't care about all that. What I mean is that whether or not they were out, she lied about where they were."

"Where were they?"

"I don't know. She said they were at the Louvre."

"Is that impossible? It may seem a little out of character, but strictly speaking, it's not impossible."

"Of course it's impossible. That was Tuesday. The Louvre was closed. I had to scratch off the Louvre and substitute the Ecclesiastical Tour, remember?"

"So you did. Well I'll be damned."

"A perfectly pointless lie, as things turned out. Of course it makes you think of a lot of things that would explain it. Well, that's the first thing on my list."

She produced a small stub of pencil, neatly sharpened, and drew a line through an item.

"Now:" she said. "René called you not long after you and Mary left, to find out why this number had been left for him to call. I told him I thought it was important but not urgent and he could probably get you or Mary here later. He said he'd be at that number until 5:30, when he was going out. I must say, he sounded very charming on the telephone."

"He would."

"Then I had a little inspiration, and called Marie Louise to ask if she knew whether René might be going out with Audrey at 5:30. She asked Audrey and Audrey said she did have the date but was afraid she was going to feel too bad to keep it. Look too bad, I imagine she really meant. So I held that in reserve. But apparently the question had got Audrey to thinking because it wasn't long after that she got worried and decided she had to tell that Louvre lie."

The pencil drew another line.

"Well, Mary called. I was glad, because I hated thinking of her sitting down there in that spooky cellar. She wanted to know if anything had happened, and I told her about Audrey saying she was with René. Mary said that was perfect. And then she asked me to tell you to arrange for René to be her escort for dinner tonight. But I thought, why not arrange it with René myself, without bothering you? And do you know what I did?"

"Surrounded him."

"No. I was mean to Audrey. I took Mary's thermometer and went up and took Audrey's temperature, which was perfectly normal, but I looked at the thermometer as if it weren't, and said to Audrey that I didn't think Dr. Finney would want her to go out. That was true as could be, of course, but had nothing to do with temperature. I practised deception, and really it wasn't necessary. I could have said the same thing without the thermometer, couldn't I? I feel I've been in Paris long enough; I'm beginning to absorb an instinct for duplicity from these people."

"Don't worry about it. It will pass. Did Audrey agree to stay in?"

"Yes, after a little hesitation. I also said a few things about how I didn't like the look of those puffs around her eyes, and a few things like that, which I think might have encouraged her in her decision to stay home."

"But Dr. Finney wants her there. She wants everybody there."

"I know. I'll reverse the decision, that's all. Then I got Marie Louise outside and half-explained things to her as much as necessary, and said I wanted her to call René and make a date with him for Mary. Naturally Marie Louise thought it was impossible, and said she didn't want to speak to René even on the telephone, but we talked about it awhile, and she changed her mind. I said, why couldn't she call and say that she had an acquaintance in town who was invited to a dinner and had to have an escort and would René oblige just as a favour to the Bellens? We worked in a few interesting suggestions as to Mary's tin and diamond holdings."

"Her—?"

"Oh, yes, she does have them. A few years ago the International Missionary United Council gave her its $1,000 award, and she brought tin and diamond stock with it. I believe René got the impression that the holdings are considerably more extensive than they are, but no actual falsehoods were told."

"Miss Collins, I'm packing you back to the honest simplicity of Africa tomorrow morning."

"I really think you had better."

"You gave poor René the impression that he was going out with a vivacious red-headed tin-and-diamond heiress."

"Oh, no, he knows that Mary is an older woman. What he has no conception of is her invulnerability. The important thing is that I did manage to make the date. He's meeting us in the foyer of the restaurant."

"At the cost of your immortal soul."

"Oh, dear," said Emmy.

I checked over the list of people who were to be Dr. Finney's guests at that dinner, and although I am not superstitious I was at least interested to note that it added up to thirteen—Marie Louise and Luigi, Audrey and René, Freddy and Bibi, Mrs. Jones and Harry, Dr. Finney and Emily Collins and Monsieur Duplin and myself, and Tony. Thirteen. I checked off those who had already been told about it, and saw that since Emmy had lured René into the deal, I had been remiss only in the cases of Mrs. Jones and Harry and Tony. I went through hell to get Mrs. Jones on the telephone but I did, and although she said that she had no intention of subjecting herself to further humiliations, I thought she sounded curious enough so that she was likely to change her mind and come to fill the place I said I would save for her. And if she came, Harry was bound to come too. But I never did get Tony. I hated to face Mary Finney with this, especially since I had had him right there that afternoon, but I just didn't have any idea how to get hold of him. The best I could do was to leave a message for Monsieur Duplin to the effect that if he had any way of getting in touch with him, which of course he would have, then he was to see that Tony got there.

Audrey told me on the telephone that she couldn't come, because that horrid little Miss Collins had told her she couldn't. I said that little Miss Collins now said she could. Audrey said all right, she'd come. Then she said, no she wouldn't, she looked too terrible. Then she said oh, all right, if I wanted her to, she would. She see-sawed around until I stopped her on a "yes she would" and we left it like that. Marie Louise got on the line and said if Dr. Finney really insisted, then all right, she herself would see that Audrey came along with her and Luigi.

Do you remember Charlie Chaplin in a picture called 'The Gold Rush'? Remember that pitiful scene where he had everything all set up for a party, and nobody came?

Well, nobody came to Mary Finney's party. Not a soul. Nobody except all the policemen, that is, and of course Emmy and me, and Monsieur Duplin.

We came into the lobby expecting to find René waiting for us, and there sat Monsieur Duplin, alone, all bright eyes and little pot belly and pressed suit with a ribbon in the lapel and, above all, all smiles. He jumped up and kissed Dr. Finney's hand—a considerable feat in itself since Jack Dempsey couldn't have been less prepared for it or more startled than Dr. Finney was—and then did the same for Emmy, who went as rigid as a poker and then seemed to turn quite limp for a moment.

Dr. Finney craned her neck in search of René as if he might be behind a chair or something of the kind, but before she could ask a question Monsieur Duplin said, "I have taken the liberty, if you please, of intercepting Monsieur Velerin-Pel." He was still smiling all over the place.

"Intercepting?" said Dr. Finney. "How come?"

I translated "how come?" for Monsieur Duplin, who then said, "It seemed most advisable, dear Doctor, that Monsieur Velerin-Pel not attend the function tonight. You must allow me to explain."

"I certainly must," Dr. Finney agreed emphatically.

"But first you must allow me to say that I have also intercepted two others of your guests. The boy and the girl. She is quite lovely, I find. And he a very handsome young man. An extremely attractive couple."

Dr. Finney stood transfixed with suspicion, but instead of asking a question she said, "Yeah."

Monsieur Duplin stood smiling until it was obvious that no one was going to say anything, and then added, completely unabashed, "And the mother was with them. Mrs. Bellen.

So naturally, it was necessary to enlarge my interception to include her."

"Most natural thing in the world," said Dr. Finney, grimly. "And I suppose something similar has happened to Mrs. Jones and Harry?"

Monsieur Duplin looked serious and sympathetic and said, "Ah, that was more complicated. The man, Harry, the lawyer, spoke to me at length concerning the best interests of his client, demanding to know what we wanted of her presence at the dinner. So naturally I told him to reassure himself. I said that it was not necessary for them to come. But the woman, who seems to be of great force, took from him the telephone and told me that of course she would come. And so it was necessary that I send a man to their place outside Neuilly to make certain that they did not. It would have been most disastrous."

"And Tony?" questioned Dr. Finney. "Did you bother to find him?"

"Ah, yes?" said Monsieur Duplin gently. "We found Tony."

Dr. Finney looked her question at him this time, and he murmured, "Yes. Quite so. Intercepted."

"My goodness," said Dr. Finney, elaborately icy, "I wonder what could be holding Freddy and Bibi?"

Now Monsieur Duplin shrugged, saying, "We tried very hard to find them this afternoon. According to the concierge of Mr. Fayerweather, he and the lady had gone shopping. My men found several shops on the Rue Ste. Honoré where this was apparently true, with the sales people in a state of great fatigue and the stocks considerably depleted, but we were not able to locate Monsieur Fayerweather and Mademoiselle Bibi themselves. But my men are stationed outside, and if Monsieur and Mademoiselle arrive, as we fully expect them to do, they will be—" and he looked at Dr. Finney with phony apology "—intercepted."

"How come you didn't intercept Hoopy here?" Mary Finney asked.

Monsieur Duplin looked at me in real surprise and said, "Alas! That I neglected to do so has robbed me, I am afraid, of the completeness of my effect."

"You did pretty well," Dr. Finney assured him. "Look, Monsieur Duplin, did something happen before or after you let me plan all this?"

"Ah! Neither before nor after, dear Doctor. Or rather, both—and during. Please, dear Doctor—and Miss Collins—and Monsieur Taliaferro—shall we ascend to the cocktails? Your audience is waiting."

We began ascending to the cocktails, but as we went Dr. Finney said, "Audience or no audience, Monsieur Duplin, I'm not going to open my mouth until you tell me what this is all about."

"It is very simple," he said. "We have, you see, discovered the murderer. Oh," he said, holding a hand up palm forward in a modest disclaimer of our surprise, "it is not entirely that we discovered the murderer. In a way the murderer discovered himself—or should I say herself?—to us. In any case, we have him. Should I say her? We have the murderer, pronouns aside. And of course the murderer would make a poor dinner guest. But if the others came, you would be disturbed by the empty place, not so? And in this way we make a most severe test of your famous acumen. Because as you talk, we, of course, know the truth."

At this point Emmy gave a small shriek, as of a lady who remembers she has left her purse in a phone booth, or something of the kind. "Professor Johnson and Bijou!" she cried.

"Professor Johnson and Bijou *what*?" asked Dr. Finney.

"I hardly know how to say it," little Emmy faltered, "but all these alibis in this case have been so—so much alike. Do you see what I mean, Mary? First Marie Louise and Luigi. Then Freddy and Bibi. Then Mrs. Jones and Tony. Then Audrey and René. And we haven't given a thought to Professor Johnson all this time. And nobody knows where Bijou is. So why not Professor Johnson and Bi—"

"Emmy, dear," said Mary Finney. That was the beginning and end of Emmy's analysis of the case.

Dr. Finney stood at the end of the room, behind our table, like a great natural monument somewhat weathered and rusted by the nagging of the elements. She had been standing there for some time, describing her way of work, and the people and some of the events—the most pertinent events—that I have set down here. The coffee had long since gone, and the brandy was almost finished. There was a lot of cigarette smoke.

"...and so I looked first at René," she said, "because the major inconsistency was his. He wanted money, and he wanted money from a woman, and the best way to get the most money from a woman was to marry her. But he didn't marry Mrs. Jones when she was begging for him, and he hadn't married Audrey when all he had to do was raise his little finger. So, I thought, the crux of the whole thing lies there. The truth is, that while I like to sort of muddle along in a case without letting myself get sold on the idea that any one person is likeliest to be the guilty one before I've muddled and muddled a lot, I couldn't help coming back to René and deciding it had to be him. But then that inconsistency got shot out from under me because Harry turned up with the information that René was married, to a girl named Gretel Gutzeit. If I'd been doing this more methodically and with more time, I'd have asked Monsieur Duplin to look up Gretel Gutzeit for me. But I suppose you did that anyway, didn't you, Monsieur Duplin?"

Monsieur Duplin grew red in the face but said nothing.

"Anyway," continued Dr. Finney, "whoever she is, Harry was able to look her up, and even to get a photograph of her. Why haven't you asked Harry, Monsieur Duplin?"

Monsieur Duplin cleared his throat uncomfortably, and said, "Until this moment, I did not know about this Gretel Gutzeit."

"I must have forgotten to mention it," Dr. Finney said. "Things have happened so fast. Well, she was a very plain girl, apparently. At least Harry and Mrs. Jones had both seen her photograph, and she said it was of a very plain girl. But sometimes, of course, a girl can change quite a bit. Bibi for instance. From a photograph of Bibi pre-Freddy, you could hardly identify Bibi post-Freddy.

"But, whoever Gretel Gutzeit was, it was obvious that Nicole knew something and I entertained the idea for a while that Nicole might have been blackmailing René. But that just added an inconsistency instead of explaining one. It was inconsistent enough that Nicole didn't drink, didn't have lovers, led a life of next to fanatic circumspection. Now if you're doing that, for whatever reason, you're not going to go in for the dangerous sport of blackmail. Nicole was a sensible, cautious, shrewd, essentially very conservative Frenchwoman intent on building a career and a profitable establishment. So I tried to forget the idea of blackmail, but I didn't forget that Nicole knew something about Gretel Gutzeit or gutzeit something, and that it was so important to her that when she was dying, and in some frightful torment of confusion, of half-delirium, what she said before she died was *gutzeit*. It was a key word, and the one that came to the surface from all the complexities and concealments that she didn't have the time or the clarity of thought to reveal to us.

"So I tried to think of some way that Nicole could have been murdered by someone named Gutzeit. Who was Bijou? Who was Tony, really? It's a German name—what about Nicole during the occupation? All that I wondered about. Suppose Audrey's name was Gutzeit before she was married. I thought about that one. It's possible to invent explanations. I invented them for all these circumstances. But I kept running into unexplained inconsistencies.

"When Mr. Taliaferro relayed Tony's story to me, I sat down to decide whether I believed it or not. It seemed perfectly reasonable to me that Tony would have gone to sit in St. Sulpice, and also that he would have gone to look at a display of his and Nicole's records in a gramophone shop, although not reasonable in cold weather. That church is an ice-box, too. I'm sure he'd done both of those things a dozen times, in good weather. And that was exactly the point. If he had wanted to invent an explanation of the way he had spent the crucial period when the murderer was in The Flea Club—and by the way, where was Bijou, since Tony had left her there?—the simple thing to do was not to invent something brand-new, but to repeat as having been true that morning, something which *had* been true on others. Much brighter than René's effort to establish an alibi by telling Audrey to claim they had been at the Louvre at that hour in the morning even if the Louvre had been open. If it had been, of course, he'd have been a safely anonymous visitor among hundreds, according to his alibi, and only its inconsistency would have been suspicious. Monsieur Duplin," she said suddenly, "you're sure you know who did this?"

"Yes," said Monsieur Duplin, with weakening conviction.

"Have you a confession?" Dr. Finney asked.

"No—not exactly a confession. We have an accusation, supported by the strongest kind of evidence."

"Have you got a motive?"

Monsieur Duplin hesitated for a long moment, and then said, "The motive you mentioned. Blackmail. It is a supposed motive. We deduce it, just as you did in the case of René. But it is not a proved motive. We do not have a motive we can prove. Not at the moment."

Dr. Finney grinned, and said, "Maybe I'll help you out yet. How's your German? What does *gutzeit* mean?"

" Jeepers!" I cried out, before I could stop. "It could mean fair weather, almost!"

Dr. Finney ignored me, while I sat there sweating for Freddy. She said, "Literally, *gut* good, *zeit* time. Or, in French, *bon temps*. Which, when you remember that Nicole's name was Marguerite Bontemps, makes the connection Gretel Gutzeit, Marguerite Bontemps. And in the disputed areas near the

Franco-German border, families have changed their names back and forth between French and German more than once. I haven't verified a thing, but I can make up a story like this:

"There was once a girl named Gretel Gutzeit who because of circumstances which are explainable in a number of ways, especially since this occurred during the disturbed years just before and at the beginning of the war, contracted a marriage with a young man well above her station, called René Velerin-Pel, as we know. It's conceivable that René could have fallen in love with Gretel. It's certainly conceivable that in love or not, he could have seduced her. It's conceivable that the marriage could have come about between the two young people in one way or another, especially given the immediate pre-war time of mobilisation and disorder. But it's most conceivable of all that René would have regretted it and insisted upon its secrecy—wrath of his family and so on—hoping to wiggle out of it some way. Then he's called to war, Gretel discovers her pregnancy, and sticks to her agreement of secrecy. She comes to Paris, and translates her German name to Marguerite Bontemps. But one thing she refuses to relinquish—her and her child's legal hold on René. Maybe she asks him for money. He can't give it to her, he's afraid to tell his family. Perhaps he finds a little money for her from time to time, and helps tide her over the first years in Paris. After the war, even with René's family bankrupt, Marguerite clings to the practical legal fact of her marriage, with all the tenacity of a woman hardened to battle with the world and unwilling to relinquish any bulwark against it. She probably keeps on getting money from René, when he had it to give, during the rough early days after the war. As both of them rise in their professions, and Marguerite Bontemps becomes Nicole, and René is in a position to acquire real money if he can divorce Marguerite and marry it, Marguerite wants her share. I'd say that she insists to René that she will give him a divorce for a certain settlement, which he is not able or not willing to meet. And all this time she is fanatically careful to lead a life of such public and indisputable decorum that René hasn't a chance to divorce her and take her child. If that is blackmail of a sort, it is not criminal blackmail. And who could ever have recognised the night-club singer Nicole as the plain little Gretel Gutzeit of the photograph? Hair bleached, eyebrows shaved and re-located, and all the glamour make-up in general.

"Then, I figured, René loses one more jackpot, Mrs. Jones, and sees himself in a position to lose what he thinks is the next best jackpot, Audrey. He's getting desperate now, and comes to see Nicole that Tuesday morning at The Flea Club—not necessarily planning to kill her, although he's wished her dead many a time—but determined to settle the business before he leaves. She is as obdurate as ever. Where is Bijou at that time? Nicole had sent Tony away because of Marie Louise and Luigi upstairs. She probably sent Bijou on an errand for the same reason. But before she can go upstairs to wake the children, René appears." Dr. Finney turned towards Monsieur Duplin and said, "You have something to fill in with here? About Tony? Because if you haven't, I think I have."

Monsieur Duplin made an indescribable gesture.

Dr. Finney went on, "You see, Tony was inconsistent too. Why did he wait so long to explain to us what he had been doing? He wasn't protecting his investment in Mrs. Jones, since he had left her long before the murder. Left her at six that morning. But when he thought she was going to stand in for him, giving him an alibi for the time of the murder, he was relieved. He didn't want to tell what he had been doing. He had some other investment to protect, and I think it could have been something like this: It's true he went to the Deux Magots; possibly he even went to St. Sulpice. But I don't think he would have had time to do both, and certainly he didn't go and stand in front of a store window he had seen before. I think he came back to The Flea Club, or started to, and saw René—if it was René—go in the cellar entrance. Nicole had got rid of Tony in a way which he himself said seemed odd to him at the time. And so, because of an instinct to spy—which after all was natural, to spy on his present mistress's ex-lover—he hung around the end of the street where he could watch inconspicuously, keeping his eye on The Flea Club's door, waiting for René to come out. He must have seen Emmy and Hoop and Professor Johnson and me go in, and then certainly he saw the police ambulance. Did he see René go out the boulevard entrance? Whether he did or not, he saw the rest of us come out, but not René, and when he learned what had happened to Nicole, he drew the obvious—and I believe the correct—conclusion."

"Why didn't he see Marie Louise and Luigi come out the boulevard door if he was so alert?" I asked.

"Because the police ambulance was at the cellar entrance taking all his attention, of course," Dr. Finney said.

I raised my hand and said, "May I say something more? I suggest that Bijou came back from her errand or whatever it was, and saw the police there too, and sank out of sight into whatever kind of place a person like Bijou can sink out of sight in, which should be almost any kind of place where there were enough people."

"Why should she want to sink out of sight? Are you entertaining the idea that Bijou had something to hide?"

"No, I'm not. I knew Bijou and you didn't, and I don't think there's a chance she had anything to hide. But it was too late for her to do anything for Nicole, and people like Bijou, really simple people who when you come down to it are at the mercy of the whole social system—where was I?—people like Bijou, I mean, are just plain afraid of the police. I think she would have let that sleeping dog lie."

"Maybe," said Dr. Finney, "except that she didn't have the chance. She did return from the errand, by the way—but earlier than your guess, and she went into The Flea Club just as usual."

"How do you know?"

"Well," said Dr. Finney, "because she's still there. This afternoon when I walked all over the place, looking into everything and trying to remember everything we did, the last thing

I did was re-visualise all that happened when we went in with Professor Johnson. The pit where we found Nicole had been about three-quarters full of earth, if you remember. I looked into it and saw it was still about half full. And for the first time I asked myself why anybody eager to dispose of Nicole in a hurry would bother to half-fill that pit before he put her in it. So I dug and—Bijou's there. Now you can figure anything you want to out of that, but I figure that when René—I always have to say *if* it was René—I figure that when René knocked Nicole on the head, not with the intention of killing her, I'm sure, but in a rage, he stood there aghast. Whether he thought he had killed her, or saw that she was still breathing—which is more probable—I don't think he would have had the idea of finishing the job by burying her alive, as we interrupted him in doing. Perhaps he planned to leave her there, to die or to be discovered. It's perfectly possible that he thought that if she recovered she wouldn't give him away—and I even think it's perfectly possible that she wouldn't have. Among possibilities we haven't even considered is the possibility that she loved the bastard. At any rate his course of action was decided for him when Bijou came in and discovered him standing there. She probably began screaming. There was only one way to cope with things now: he strangled Bijou. It was a quick, easy job for a strong and desperate man. He put her in the pit and threw in enough earth to cover the body thoroughly. What is he doing? Hiding her from Nicole, if Nicole recovers? I think it is at this point that he takes the cash out of the box and throws the box into the pit with Bijou, taking double advantage of getting away with a considerable sum of money, and hoping to present a misleading motive for the crime. Although I doubt that he thought of it rationally. We can think of René by this time as acting in a state close to hysteria. Frantic, clutching at any straw that suggests concealment, he dumps Nicole into the pit anti begins to cover her, too, with earth, and he is in that process when he hears us coming, and leaves things as we found them.

"Monsieur Duplin, I'm not certain just how you found René or who accused him, but I'm betting on Tony. But even without Tony, René would have given himself away eventually. He had already made one bad mistake. He had asked Audrey to supply him with an alibi for that morning, protesting his complete innocence, of course, and depending on her abject enslavement to make her accept whatever flimsy reasons he presented to her. And if Audrey has been a woman in hell, which she certainly has, it has been as much her suspicion of René's guilt as the discovery of his marriage."

Dr. Finney sighed heavily and turned to Monsieur Duplin. "I should have called you right away about finding Bijou," she admitted, "but if you want to prosecute me for concealment or something I plead for leniency on the grounds of a rushed schedule and only a slight delay. I only found her—" she looked at her watch—"a little more than four hours ago." Sighing again, she said, "Well, it's always fun until you catch them, then you're awfully let down. I hate to see even a son-of-a-bitch in such bad trouble. Am I right, Monsieur Duplin? Is it René?"

Monsieur Duplin rose, and Dr. Finney sat down. "Yes," he said, "René." He spoke deliberately, saying, "The Sûreté does not release a Tony as easily as I appeared to do this afternoon. He was of course followed. It did not take him long to go to René's rooms. He went first to his own quarters, and there no doubt he picked up the knife, which of course he did not have when we released him and returned to him his things. Nor had he any money at that time—a little odd change left from whatever Nicole had advanced him. Certainly he went to René and demanded money for the concealment of his knowledge that René entered and left The Flea Club that morning. We arrived in time, possibly, to save Tony's life. René of course claims that Tony attacked him with the knife, and that thus he was forced to shoot him. It is a stomach wound. Tony denies the attack, and truly there would have been no reason, except his own defence. René—who has been intercepted—does not know that Tony has told us he saw René at The Flea Club that morning. For a conviction we would have only the word of Tony—except that now, dear Doctor, you have also given us a motive, as well as the corpse of the woman Bijou. The affair, I believe, can be called settled."

The three of us—Dr. Finney, Emily Collins, and I—sat at a table along the Champs-Elysées, not having felt like going to the general vicinity of The Flea Club for a nightcap after the dinner. We found little to say, and I bought a newspaper. I always read the horoscopes, and I asked Dr. Finney if she would like hers. "Sure," she said. "Sign of the Fish."

Under Pisces it said, "Look forward soon to an interruption of the tranquillity of your life. Make new friends cautiously, and do not travel long distances. Stick conscientiously to your own work, avoiding distractions. Furthermore," I went on, as if still reading, "go home and get a little sleep, and give old friends from Africa a chance to do likewise. O.K.?"

"O.K.," said Mary Finney.